BONE-CHILLING TALES
OF FRIGHT

BONE-CHILLING TALES OF FRIGHT

Lowell 🏠 House
Juvenile
Los Angeles

CONTEMPORARY BOOKS
Chicago

Library of Congress Catalogue Card Number: 94-30325
ISBN: 1-56565-167-7

Publisher: Jack Artenstein
General Manager, Juvenile Division: Elizabeth D. Wood
Editorial Director: Brenda Pope-Ostrow
Director of Publishing Services: Mary D. Aarons
Project Editor: Barbara Schoichet
Cover Designer: Lisa-Theresa Lenthall
Text Designer: Tim Slavin

Illustration Credits:
Brian Dow—pp. 8, 59, and 102
Steven Murashige—p. 18
Damian Valentine Mayek—pp. 27 and 91
Bernard Custodio—p. 50
Wendy Chang—pp. 78 and 111

Manufactured in the United States of America
10 9 8 7 6 5 4 3 2 1

Contents

NATURE'S WAY

By Q. L. Pearce

JUST LOOK AT this mess! Somebody's going to trip on one of these things and break his neck." Devon's mother kicked aside several large, plastic dinosaurs that were threatening each other in the hallway.

"Aw, Mom," Devon complained. "We weren't finished playing with them yet."

"Well, I'm tired of stepping over them. Why don't you and your sister go play in your room...or outside? It's such a lovely day. You shouldn't be lazing around in the house, getting in my way. That's why I never get anything done. And heaven forbid someone should offer to help me with the housework on occasion, instead of just making more mess."

Devon sighed and glanced at his younger sister, Annette. As their mom walked away, still muttering angrily, they started to retrieve the plastic dinosaurs that were scattered across the floor. With a scowl, Devon picked up a fierce-looking *Tyrannosaurus rex* and threw it at the wall. Annette did the same with a long-necked *Apatosaurus*.

"C'mon," Devon grumbled. "I was tired of playing with the stupid things anyway." His sister followed him to the den and flopped down beside him as he switched on the television set. The wailing sound of a police siren filled the room. A bad guy on the screen was waving a remote-control device of some sort and threatening to blow up the city hall unless his demands were met.

"Can't you kids turn that volume down?!" Devon's dad complained from behind the sports section of his newspaper. "I don't work hard all week long so that I can spend my Sundays listening to that junk."

Devon switched off the television and flashed a meaningful look at his little sister. They both jumped up and headed for the front door.

Outside, Devon searched the ground for a moment, then picked up a small, smooth rock and rubbed it between his thumb and forefinger. He pulled a slingshot from his back pocket and dropped the rock into the rubber pouch. Devon looked around searching for a target, then he smiled.

"Watch this," he told Annette. He closed one eye, raised the loaded weapon, and aimed it at their next-door neighbor's mailbox. Then he let the rock fly. It hit the box with a loud clang.

His sister nodded in approval. "Now it's my turn," she said, excitedly waving the shiny new slingshot Devon had given her for her birthday. Devon helped her to pick a good rock, one that was round and smooth and fit perfectly into the sling. He showed her how to steady her thumb against her cheek as she drew the sling back. But at the last moment, she nervously closed her eyes when she let go, and the shot was too wide. The rock missed the mailbox by at least a foot and shattered a small pot of geraniums beside the fence.

2

"Amateur," Devon teased.

The door to the neighbor's house flew open, and Mr. Davis came out on the front step.

"You kids get away from here!" he shouted angrily. "I'm getting tired of your nonsense. Do I have to call your parents again?" And then he noticed the broken pot. "You two will have to pay for that!" he yelled and started toward them.

Laughing and making faces, Devon and Annette ran down the street toward the park. They slowed to a walk on the next block, then stopped to watch Mrs. Wareham in her garden. The elderly woman was on her knees, digging in the soil at the edge of a bed of periwinkles. She always seemed to be working out there, tending her flowers or filling one of the dozen or so bird feeders she kept. Her yard was regularly teeming with birds, squirrels, and other small animals.

"Look at that," Devon whispered with a nasty grin. "It looks like she's burying something. Probably the results of a spell that didn't work."

Annette looked up at him trustingly. "Do you really think so? That seems kind of strange to me. Why would she bury something during the day, and out in the open like this, where anyone could see?"

Devon rolled his eyes. "To avoid suspicion. Don't you know anything?"

"I don't think she's really a witch," Annette said, frowning. "I think she's just a weird old lady."

"That's because you're just a little kid. You haven't seen all the things that I have." Devon turned away so his sister wouldn't notice him trying to stifle a laugh. "And I don't hang around with little kids," he added, a smile creeping across his face just before he broke into a run. "Look," he shouted. "I think Old Lady Wareham is coming this way!"

"Wait!" Annette shrieked, and took off after him.

THE FOLLOWING DAY, Devon had to stay after school because he had dumped Randy Carson's lunch out on the playground and called him a few unkind names. Annette walked home alone. She slowed as she passed Mrs. Wareham's garden. There was a new birdbath right in the center of one of the colorful petunia beds. A small, blue, ceramic bird was perched on the edge of the bath, as though it were taking a drink. Annette smiled.

"Devon would be really impressed if I could hit that," she said to herself. Looking from side to side to be sure that no one was watching, she pulled her slingshot from her book bag and loaded it with a small rock. Pulling back and steadying the sling just as he had taught her, Annette released her ammunition. The rock sailed across the street and narrowly missed a real bird that was pecking at a crust of bread.

"Not even close," Annette grumbled in frustration.

"On the contrary."

The voice came from behind her. Annette whirled around and came face to face with Mrs. Wareham. The woman was wheeling a little luggage cart that held a couple of bags of groceries. "If you meant to hit the bird, you were almost on target."

The little girl backed up a step. "No. I didn't mean to hurt anything."

Mrs. Wareham frowned and said nothing for a moment. Annette felt her hands begin to tremble. What if the old woman really was a witch? Was she about to cast a spell?

"If you continue to shoot at things with that sling-shot," Mrs. Wareham said finally, "something or someone is bound to get hurt, and it might not be who you expect. Nature has a way of taking care of itself." Her eyes flashed angrily. "There are spirits that live all around us, within every tree, every flower, and every growing thing. And there are guardians whose only purpose is to protect the natural world." She paused. "I'm warning you, child. If you willingly inflict pain, nature has a way of settling things."

Annette continued to back fearfully away. Then she noticed Devon, who was taking his usual shortcut through the park across the street. "Look," she whimpered, "I'm really sorry, okay? I see my brother. He's probably looking for me. I gotta go." She made a wide circle around the woman, then fled into the park.

"Devon," Annette gasped as she reached him. "You won't believe what happened. Old Lady Wareham snuck up on me and had me cornered. You were right. She really *is* a witch. She was going to turn me into something horrible…a toad or something. I just barely got away!"

"Wait a minute. Slow down," Devon said, laughing. "What are you trying to tell me? You really think Old Lady Wareham is a witch?"

"She *is!*" the frightened girl insisted. "She told me she was going to cast a spell on me and turn me into a newt because I almost hit one of her birds with a rock!" The more Annette embellished the story, the harder her brother laughed.

"You're crazy," he howled. "Old Lady Wareham is nothing more than that—an old lady!"

Annette blushed. She was beginning to get angry. "You're the one who told me she was a witch!"

"I just said that to scare you," Devon chuckled, wiping the tears from his eyes. "And it sure worked. Look at you! What a little scaredy-cat."

"Well," Annette pouted, "if I'm afraid of her, then I'll bet you are, too."

"I am not," Devon shot back, crossly.

She realized she had annoyed him and pressed the point. "Oh, really? I've never seen you try to shoot anything in her yard. What's the matter? You scared?" she sneered. "You boast about it, but I've never seen you do it."

The smile vanished from Devon's face and was replaced by a scowl. "Well, just watch me, then." He tugged out his slingshot, loaded it, and trotted to within striking distance of Mrs. Wareham's garden.

"Aim at the little blue statue over there on the birdbath," Annette whispered.

"I'll do better than that," he bragged. "See the bird on that branch...?" He pulled back the sling, let go, and watched the course of the rock. It hit the small bird with full force. The little creature crumpled lifelessly to the ground.

Annette gasped. Even Devon was surprised. He hadn't truly intended to kill it.

The door to the house opened, and Mrs. Wareham stepped out onto the lawn. She knelt and gently lifted the frail, feathered body in her hand. Then she looked up toward where Annette and Devon were standing. They ducked quickly behind a hedge.

"Stay low!" Devon whispered. "I'm afraid she can see us."

The old woman stroked the dead bird with the tips of her fingers. For a second, Devon felt a sharp, shooting pain in his side that made him wince.

At last, Mrs. Wareham turned and walked slowly back inside, still cradling the tiny victim.

THAT NIGHT, DEVON was awakened from a sound sleep with the unsettling feeling that he was being watched. He stared out into the darkened room. Everything was still and quiet.

Then, all at once, there was a noise—a fluttering sound—at the window. The drapes were open, and there was a full moon high in the sky, allowing Devon to see that there was nothing there. Shrugging, he rolled over to go back to sleep. Then he heard it again. This time, Devon rose and quietly padded to the window. He leaned against the glass and looked out in all directions...nothing. But when he turned to go back to bed, fear struck his heart like an icy blade. On the wall over his bed was the shadow of a large bird. Its wings were arched, and its knifelike talons were spread open for attack.

"Dad! Mom!" Devon screamed, as he dropped to his knees and cowered in a corner.

A moment later, the light flicked on and his bewildered parents were standing in his room. "It's after me!" Devon sobbed. "I saw its shadow there on the wall!"

"What are you talking about?" his father asked, slightly irritated for having been startled awake.

Devon ran to the switch and turned out the light. "There!" He pointed to the shadow over his bed. But somehow it didn't look the same.

"So what?" his father said, definitely irritated now. "It's the shadow of a tree limb. Is that what you woke us up for?"

Devon stared at the dark silhouette. It had changed. "I guess I made a mistake," he mumbled.

"And because of that the whole family has to lose sleep?" his father complained. "I have a big meeting tomorrow, and I need my rest."

"Don't worry. I won't bother you again," Devon said quietly. Feeling foolish, he watched his parents leave, then, with one last look outside, he drew the drapes across his window. He slipped into bed and tried to go back to sleep.

THE NEXT DAY at school, Devon once again had the creepy feeling that he was being watched. No matter how he tried, he couldn't shake it. He couldn't concentrate during class, and he ate his lunch alone. As soon as the final bell rang, he grabbed his jacket and left school without waiting for Annette.

As he stepped through the schoolyard gate and headed toward home, he heard something stirring in the dense hedge by the sidewalk. Devon stopped and tried to peer into the dark, leafy shadows.

"It's just a mouse or something," he said, under his

breath. "There's nothing to be afraid of." But he quickened his pace to a trot.

He was halfway across the almost-deserted park when he felt the first peck on the side of his head. Something had struck him. In panic, he looked from one end of the park to the other, but he saw nothing. With a whack, something hit him hard on the shoulder. He whirled around to fight it off...but there was nothing there.

"Where are you!?" Devon cried. "What do you want?"

In answer, he heard a loud screech from above. Although he couldn't see his attackers, he could hear the flurry of wings and feel the pain of beaks and claws as they dug into his skin.

"Leave me alone," he wailed, covering his head with his arms and running blindly to escape his invisible tormentors.

Suddenly, he slammed at full speed into the six-foot-high chain-link fence that marked the south end of the park. Gripping the links, he tried to clamber over the fence. Then, all at once, the attack ended. For a moment Devon felt relief...until he glimpsed a shadow circling on the ground. Still clinging to the fence, he turned his gaze upward and saw a beautiful bird with gold-flecked eyes. The bird was descending toward him faster and faster. With a shriek, Devon lost his grip, tumbled to the ground, and blacked out.

WHEN HE CAME to, Devon was looking into the same gold-flecked eyes, but from a different angle.

"Don't worry, little one," someone soothed him. "You

will be well cared for…a life for a life."

Slowly, Devon became aware that he'd heard that voice before. But where? And then he realized whose eyes he was gazing into—they belonged to Mrs. Wareham. But she was *below* him, and he was looking *down* at her.

"Nature has a way of settling things," she continued gently. "I told your little sister that. I told her all about us. Of course I didn't tell her that I, too, was a guardian."

In spite of the old woman's calming tone, Devon was terrified. All he wanted to do was run…to get away. But instead of running, he felt himself rising. He glanced down at his body and tried to scream. But Devon could no longer form words, for he was no longer a boy—but a bird. Wheeling high in the sky, Devon dove in terror, as he suddenly felt a searing pain in one wing. Blood seeped across the edge of his flight feathers, and he looked down to see Annette loading her slingshot again.

"Wait until I tell Devon," he heard her say as he plummeted toward the earth. "He'll be so impressed that my aim is improving."

POST-MORTEM

By Don Wulffson

THE LAST YEAR had been filled with nothing but heartache for 14-year-old Stacy Linden and her mother. First, there had been the divorce. The divorce had left Stacy, her mother, and her Grandma Doris to get by as best they could, living together in a small rented house on meager welfare and Social Security benefits.

The worst blow had been the sudden death of her grandmother. Stacy had adored the kindly old lady. For Stacy's mother, the shock of suddenly finding herself without either her husband or her mother had been more than she could bear. Often, she stayed in bed all day or shuffled listlessly about the house in her robe.

In June, things had taken a turn for the better. Stacy had gotten a summer job at the law firm of Hartridge and Meyer. She did little more than run errands and file papers, but it was a new beginning and a place away from all the unhappiness at home. Stacy liked the people she worked with. She liked the feeling of being on her own, of being independent, and of earning some money. And since she and her mother needed the money so badly, it made her feel good about herself that she could help out.

For a time, even her mother started to snap out of it, to come to terms with her grief. She took an interest in fixing up their little house, and she even got a part-time job, doing piecework at home as a seamstress.

For the first time in a very, very long time, Stacy began to feel happy. Things were looking up, and Stacy was certain they would only get better. Finally, the future seemed filled with hope and promise.

And then came a phone call at work.

"Stacy, there's a call for you on line one," Mr. Bradshaw, an associate lawyer, told her. "It's your mother. She sounds upset."

A bit worried, Stacy picked up the phone. The voice on the other end of the line sounded like a woman gone mad. Her words made no sense. Her mother cried, then babbled something about a letter—"from your Grandma Doris." At first Stacy was not sure what her mother was talking about. Had her mom come across an old letter from Grandma—one that brought back painful memories?

"No, it's not an *old* letter!" her mother sobbed hysterically. "You don't understand! You don't understand at all!"

Stacy tried to question her further, but her mother began sobbing and was unable to continue. There was a loud click as she hung up.

Not until she got home that evening, anxious and troubled, did Stacy begin to understand.

"I found this on my desk!" cried her mother, waving a piece of pink stationery in Stacy's face. Stacy took the paper and read out loud: *"I'm so lonely, my darling, so lost without you. Come to me."* The message was written in

what looked like her grandmother's flowery handwriting
…but it *couldn't* be.

"There's no date," Stacy pointed out. "When do you
think it was written?"

Her mother sat down. Her face was a tight, twisted
mask. She began rocking back and forth.

"Mom," Stacy coaxed. "Try to think. Do you have
any idea when this could have been written?"

The answer was a wailing shriek. "Today!" her mother screeched, continuing to rock, tugging and twisting at
a lock of her hair.

"That's not possible, Mother," said Stacy as evenly as
she could. "I'm sure it's some sort of—" She struggled to
find the right word. "Just some sort of *mistake.*"

Her mother shook her head violently. "There's no
mistake about it. This letter was written today."

Stacy put a hand on her mother's shoulder. "Grandma
didn't write that letter, at least not today. She's dead,
Mom. Grandma is dead."

Her mother stared into space. "Yes," she said, her
voice a hollow monotone. "But the dead never leave us."

"Mother—!"

"Don't you see?" her mother interrupted, taking
Stacy's hand. "She's trying to communicate with me, to
reach me. She needs me, Stacy. My mother needs me!"

"But Grandma's dead!" Stacy blurted, fighting the
fear rising within her.

Her mother smiled strangely. "But she's calling out to me."

Stacy put her arms around her mother. "You're lonely,
Mom. I understand because I'm lonely, too. This has been
hard on both of us. But we can't let it get to us, or make

us imagine things." She forced a smile. "Mom, dead people don't write letters."

Her mother just looked at her with an odd, faraway look in her eyes.

BUT WITH EACH passing day, things became worse. More ugly. More insane.

Almost unbearable.

There were more letters from her grandmother. And more phone calls to Stacy at work from her mother. The calls shattered her nerves, often leaving her in tears.

The calls and the change in Stacy's behavior did not go unnoticed by her fellow workers.

One day, after her mother had called three times, the floor manager, Ms. Trump, took Stacy aside. "I don't mean to pry into your personal life," she said, "nor do I really understand what's going on. But these phone calls from your mother are interfering with your work."

Stacy apologized and promised the calls would stop.

Which they did—when Stacy demanded that her mother leave her alone at work. That's when things at home got worse.

Now, every day when Stacy came home she was greeted by a crazy woman. A woman who sometimes ranted and raved. Or sat hunched over, reading and rereading letters on pink stationery. Letters supposedly from her Grandma Doris, who was dead and buried but somehow still with them, now as a dark and sinister part of their lives.

With each day, Stacy's heart broke again when she walked in the house and saw her mother. The poor woman ate almost nothing. Her bones showed. Her back was bent over more and more each day. Her face became pale and waxy looking. Her eyes, sunken and vacant looking, were forever moving restlessly, as if looking for someone—for Grandma Doris, to appear.

Always complaining of one ailment or another, her mother had quit her work as a seamstress, too, and returned to her old ways. Once again she stayed in bed most of the day or wandered about in her shabby robe, her pockets stuffed with dozens of letters on pink stationery.

Stacy begged her to go see a doctor, to get help. But the pleas had only brought on fits of yelling and tears, followed by long hours of torturous, icy silence.

Only at work did Stacy find any peace. Only there did she have any purpose, any freedom from the ugliness of her home life. She felt guilty, but she no longer wanted to go home. As often as she could, she volunteered to work overtime.

Late one afternoon, the last bit of normalcy left Stacy's life. She would never forget how the whole office plunged into silence when the doors burst open and her mother, clad in her robe and slippers, stormed in. Her hair hung in dirty ringlets. Her fevered, glassy eyes searched out—then riveted on—Stacy. As her mother came toward her, Stacy wanted to run, to hide, to pretend she didn't know her.

Stacy's face was red with embarrassment, and tears were in her eyes. Her mother stood before her, pulled a pink paper from her robe, and read: *"Your mother needs you. Come to me. Come to me now!"*

Two secretaries said something in an undertone.

Someone coughed. Then, seemingly startled, as though realizing for the first time where she was, her mother gathered her robe about herself and she stared, wide-eyed, at the stunned office workers. Then she turned and walked back through the silent office and out the door.

Stacy ran to the ladies' room to cry...and to hide.

Stacy did not wait to be fired. She quit that afternoon. The embarrassment of it all was just too great. She could never show her face there again.

Instead of taking the bus home that horrible day, Stacy walked all the way home. It was a good five miles and the evening was hot and very humid. She was exhausted and sticky with perspiration when she finally got home.

All was dark and strangely still in the house. "Mother!" she called out. There was no reply. Stacy made her way from room to room, flipping on lights as she went.

She found her mother sitting at her desk in her bedroom, her back to the door.

"Why, Mother?" Stacy asked. "Why did you do that to me?"

Her mother remained motionless.

Filled with sorrow and compassion, Stacy's anger drained from her. She walked over and put a hand on her mother's shoulder. The swivel chair turned and her mother slumped to one side, her glazed eyes fixed on some distant point. She was dead. "Mother!" Stacy screamed, again and again and again.

ON THE WAY back from the funeral, the lady from child welfare department talked about Stacy's future and about the

McLeish Home for Girls, where Stacy would be staying until foster parents could be found for her. Or, Mrs. Canfield had wondered aloud, "Perhaps some arrangement can be worked out with your father?"

Stacy shook her head. "No, I'm better off without him. He doesn't care about me any more than he cared about my mother. He wasn't even at the funeral!"

Mrs. Canfield looked uncomfortable. "I don't know all the details, but I can see you've been through a lot." She smiled at Stacy warmly. "Things will start looking up—you'll see."

Stacy brushed back a tear. "I'll be okay," she said in a slightly quavering voice.

At the house, Mrs. Canfield helped Stacy tote two suitcases and several boxes of belongings out to the car. On the way to the McLeish Home for Girls, Mrs. Canfield stopped and treated Stacy to a lunch. Afterward, they went for a walk together in the park. Stacy liked Mrs. Canfield. She told her all about what had happened—about her grandmother, her mother, and about the letters and her mother's going mad. "My mom's at peace now," she said.

————

THE FOLLOWING WEEK, Mrs. Canfield and Stacy returned to the house. New renters would be moving in, and something would have to be done with her mother's clothing and other belongings. Except for a few keepsakes, Stacy decided everything should go to charity. Together, she and Mrs. Canfield stacked boxes on the front porch.

It was dark and dusky by the time they finished, and Mrs. Canfield sat down on the porch stairs to rest.

Stacy went back into the house to take one last look around. All was so quiet, so deathly quiet. Especially her mother's bedroom. The place sent chills down her spine. But a few last things now had to be done . . . including cleaning out that desk.

Stacy left the pencils, pens, erasers, and paper clips where she had found them in the top drawer. In another drawer she found magazines, newspaper clippings, and a few old photographs. She put the photographs in her purse, and the rest went into the wastebasket.

But it was the bottom drawer that took all of Stacy's willpower to clean. From it she pulled a half-empty box of stationery and a stack of papers. Most were letters, the letters that had driven her mother mad.

Tears fell from Stacy's eyes as, one by one, she tore up the letters and threw them into the wastebasket.

The blank stationery frightened and upset her as much as the letters. She hated it, wanted to be rid of it, to be done, once and for all, with every last reminder of the insanity that had destroyed her mother. She grabbed the box, and suddenly she was overcome with grief. Her hands shook violently. "Mother!" she cried. "No!" The box fell from her hands, and pink stationery scattered across the desktop.

A voice came from far away, from outside. "Stacy, we'd better get a move on," Mrs. Canfield called from somewhere out front.

For a moment Stacy's head cocked in the direction of Mrs. Canfield's voice. Then she glanced back at the desk.

"Stacy?" called the faint voice.

But Stacy said nothing. She gripped the armrest of the chair, her eyes fixed on a pink sheet of stationery.

The handwriting was tight, and cramped looking. It was her mother's writing. Slowly, words formed across the background of pink. "No," Stacy whispered. "Mother, please, no."

Mrs. Canfield rushed into the room. "What's wrong?" she asked. "Are you all right?"

Stacy's gaze traveled slowly from the piece of stationery to Mrs. Canfield. Slowly, Stacy handed the woman the pink piece of paper.

Mrs. Canfield read out loud: *"Now you understand, my darling daughter. I miss you so much, love you so much. Come to me, my love, please come."*

"Stacy, did you write this?" asked Mrs. Canfield. "Stacy? Stacy!" Mrs. Canfield began to shake her. "Stacy, who wrote this?"

But Stacy said nothing. She looked up at the woman. Her face slowly twisted into an odd smile. Her eyes were glassy, filled with horror. And the dawning of madness.

THE POLTERGEIST
By Sandra K. Bailey

STEPHANIE AND HER twin sister, Kerry, were organizing storage boxes in the garage of their family's new home, a recently restored Victorian built in the 1850s.

"I wish we knew more about this old house," Stephanie said as she climbed a ladder to shove a box onto an upper shelf. "Some of these old houses around here are supposed to have secret passageways that they used to hide runaway slaves before the Civil War.

Kerry's eyes lit up. "Really?" She paused and thought for a moment. "For all we know, somebody famous might have lived here."

"Maybe when we get to know the neighbors, they'll be able to tell us something," Stephanie said, climbing down the ladder and walking out of the garage. "Hey, look," she said excitedly. "Over by that old tree. Maybe she's here to welcome us to the neighborhood."

Kerry turned and looked off across the lawn toward a huge, old oak tree that dominated the landscape. A young girl about their age was standing under its boughs.

"Look at the way she's dressed," Kerry said, grimacing at the long dress the girl was wearing. "I hope all the kids around here don't dress like that."

"Maybe she's going to a party," Stephanie suggested. "C'mon, let's go meet her."

As the twins approached the girl under the tree, they could see that her dress wasn't only unfashionably long, but strangely ornamented and antique looking. The way she wore her hair was unusual, too. Stephanie called out a "hello" and waved to the girl, but instead of answering or waving back, the girl stared at the twins sullenly and didn't say a word. Unnerved by her manner, Stephanie and Kerry stopped a few feet away.

"Maybe she's deaf, or something," Kerry whispered.

Stephanie nodded, then raised her voice and tried again. "I'm Stephanie Cross," she said slowly and distinctly in case the girl was lip-reading. She pointed to Kerry. "This is my sister, Kerry."

Kerry started to smile, but a glint of cold hatred in the strange girl's eyes stopped her. Stephanie simply assumed the girl was scared of strangers. "You don't have to be afraid of us," Stephanie continued loudly in case the girl hadn't heard. "Are you our neighbor?"

At that, the girl smiled, but it was a strangely cruel smile that sent shivers down Kerry's spine.

"I'm Maureen," the girl said. "I saw you move in. And you don't have to shout. I can hear everything you say."

The twins exchanged a glance, surprised that anyone who could hear and speak normally would have behaved so rudely.

Maureen looked from one twin to the other. "You're

exactly alike," she observed.

"No. I'm older," Stephanie volunteered proudly.

"Do you live around here?" Kerry asked, beginning to hope that she didn't.

Maureen smiled that same cruel smile. "Yes," she said, "I live very close by." She looked away toward the house as if that were what interested her, not the twins.

While Maureen's head was turned, Kerry nudged Stephanie, mouthed the word "weird," and tapped her head. Stephanie nodded in agreement, then shrugged.

The three girls continued to stand there in awkward silence until Stephanie couldn't stand it any longer and made an effort to revive the conversation. "Would you like to see our room?" she asked, forcing herself to sound like she meant it. "We finally got everything put away just where we want it."

"Why not?" Maureen smirked.

The rude way she said it and the look she gave the girls made Kerry uneasy. She looked at Stephanie to see if her sister had picked up on the ill will Maureen obviously felt toward them, but, as usual, Stephanie didn't have a clue.

"Great," Stephanie said, sounding as though she meant it. She eagerly led the way to the house with Maureen only a few steps behind her. Kerry held back a moment, watching them go, trying to put her finger on exactly what it was about Maureen that disturbed her.

––––––––––––

"OH, NO!" STEPHANIE exclaimed as she opened the door to their bedroom.

Kerry looked in the room and gasped. The entire room, which she and Stephanie had organized so carefully half an hour ago, was now a shambles. Books, dolls, pictures—everything was lying helter-skelter on the floor.

"How could this have happened?" Stephanie wailed. She waded through the piles of possessions and picked up her favorite stuffed animal. One of its ears was partly torn off. She held it up for Kerry to see. "Look." There were tears in her eyes.

Kerry picked up a book lying near the door. The cover was torn loose at one end. A tide of anger welled up inside her. Why would anyone do such a mean, senseless thing? She turned to show the book to Maureen.

The odd girl had vanished.

———

STEPHANIE AND KERRY left everything just as it was until their mother returned from work that evening. Mrs. Cross stood in the doorway of the room and surveyed the mess, then turned a stern look on her daughters. "You're sure this isn't one of your pranks?" she asked.

"We spent all day putting things away," Stephanie objected. "Why would we mess it up?"

"Because someone told you about the poltergeist. That's why," their mother said.

"Poltergeist? What's a poltergeist?" the twins said in unison.

Mrs. Cross searched their confused expressions. She could never tell when the twins were lying. This time, however, they seemed to be sincere.

"A poltergeist," she began, "is a restless spirit who

makes its presence known by throwing things or moving them around."

"Like a ghost?" Kerry asked disbelievingly.

Her mother nodded.

Stephanie shivered. "Are you saying our house is haunted?"

"Absolutely not," Mrs. Cross said with finality. "But according to the man who restored the house, strange things happen here sometimes. For example, while he was working, tools would disappear, paint cans would tip over, but nothing like this," she said, eyeing the room with concern. "This is taking things too far."

"But if there is a poltergeist…" Stephanie began.

Her mother held up a hand to silence her. "Your father and I discounted that silly rumor the first time we heard it. No, what we have here is an ordinary human vandal."

"Maybe Maureen saw who did it," Stephanie said. "She was standing outside."

"Maureen?" Mrs. Cross asked.

"A girl we met today," Kerry explained. "She was with us when it happened."

Kerry wondered if she should tell her mother about the hostility Maureen seemed to feel toward them, but decided against it.

"Well, I doubt a little girl could do all this," Mrs. Cross said, looking sadly at the room. "But what kind of a mean-spirited person *could* do something like this?"

"Do you think we ought to call Dad?" Stephanie asked.

"There's not much he can do from the other side of the world," Mrs. Cross responded. "Besides, when he's away on business, I don't want to disturb him. I think this is something for the sheriff to handle anyway." Suddenly, her manner abruptly changed. Eyeing the girls with suspicion, she asked, "Why did you suggest we call your father?"

Stephanie shrugged, "Well, this is kind of scary and..."

"This isn't another of your plots to bring your father home early?" her mother challenged.

Stephanie and Kerry exchanged an outraged look. "Mom!" they objected.

Mrs. Cross eyed the girls critically for a moment, then sighed and smiled apologetically. "I'm sorry, but the last time you cried wolf, it caused your father and me a lot of trouble. We can't afford to go through that again."

SHERIFF TUTTLE ARRIVED within minutes of Mrs. Cross's call. Even as he surveyed the mess in the girls' room, he confessed he wasn't very hopeful. "In cases like these, it's hard to be optimistic," he said. "I'll send somebody out tomorrow to dust for fingerprints, but with this kind of mess, getting a clean set won't be easy. Your best bet is to keep watch and let me know if you see anybody suspicious hanging around."

"There's Maureen," Kerry blurted out.

"Maureen?" the sheriff asked.

Mrs. Cross shook her head. "It couldn't be her. She was with the girls when their room was trashed."

"What do you know about this girl?" Officer Tuttle asked.

Stephanie and Kerry shrugged. "Just that her name is Maureen."

"And she's really weird," Kerry added.

"Weird, how?" the sheriff asked.

Kerry shrugged. "Not in any particular way, just weird."

The sheriff sighed. "Well, next time you see her, get her full name and phone number. I'd like to talk to her."

"We will," the twins chorused.

Since their room was still a mess, Stephanie and Kerry had to sleep in the big bed in the guest room that night. Stephanie slept deeply, but Kerry tossed and turned, sweating in her sleep. *"Wake up! Wake up!"* a voice inside her head kept urging. *"Wake up, Kerry. Hurry!"*

Kerry had never felt so helpless. She knew she had to wake up, but no matter how hard she tried, she couldn't break through the blanket of sleep that lay heavily over her.

"Wake up, Kerry!" The voice was screaming now.

Making a superhuman effort, Kerry forced herself awake. At first, she thought she was still dreaming. Anything that wasn't nailed down was flying around the room, colliding with one another, and tumbling down around her and Stephanie. Kerry watched in frozen amazement for a moment, then saw that the bureau next to the bed was rocking back and forth. Stephanie was still asleep. If the bureau fell forward, it would crush her.

"Stephanie, wake up!" Kerry shouted. Jumping out of bed, she yanked her sister to the floor.

An instant later, the bureau crashed onto the bed right where Stephanie had been sleeping. Kerry screamed. Abruptly, everything that had been flying around stopped moving and fell to the floor.

Kerry's scream brought Mrs. Cross running into the room. She switched on the light, then paused in the door-way for a moment, stunned by the disorder. "Stephanie! Kerry!" she shouted. "Where are you?"

"Here, Mom. We're all right," Kerry's frightened voice reassured her as she and Stephanie got up from where they hid on the other side of the bed. Stephanie was fully awake now and crying.

Mrs. Cross hugged the girls close to her. "Are you all right? Do you know what happened?"

"It was so scary," Kerry said, tears welling in her eyes. "I was having this weird dream, like I was tied up or some-thing. Then I knew I had to wake up, but something wouldn't let me. Finally, I did manage to wake up, and I saw everything flying all around the room. Then, the bureau started to fall and I pulled Stephanie out of bed." She looked at Stephanie. "I can't believe you slept through the whole thing!"

Mrs. Cross stepped away from the girls and studied them carefully. "Now, Kerry," she began, "you and I both know nothing could have been flying around the room."

"But I *saw* it," Kerry protested.

Mrs. Cross looked from one girl to the other. They certainly *looked* scared. But the twins missed their father. They had gone to extreme measures to bring him home before and were apparently capable of doing so again. No one could have sneaked in and done the damage she was looking at while the twins slept.

"You two must think I'm either stupid, or impossibly gullible," she said sternly. "And, I'll admit, I believed you this afternoon—but this!" She stopped, too angry to continue.

31

Kerry and Stephanie exchanged a look.

"We'll discuss it in the morning," their mother said. "And I would suggest you start thinking of some way to apologize to Sheriff Tuttle for wasting his time." Still furious, she righted the bureau so that Stephanie could get back in the bed, and walked out of the room.

The next morning, the girls' mother wouldn't listen to anything they tried to say in their defense. In fact, until they confessed, they were grounded.

"So what are we going to do?" Stephanie asked Kerry later while they were cleaning up their room. Their mother had gone out shopping and was expecting a confession when she got back.

Kerry shrugged, plopped down on the window seat, and gazed wearily outside. "We could always confess, but then, if the poltergeist does something else, Mom'll just think it's us and punish us again. What we need to do is get rid of it somehow." She sat there and thought a moment, then hopped up to her feet. "I know," she cried. "Maureen! *She* knows what's going on. I'm sure of it. C'mon, let's go find her."

MAUREEN WAS IN her usual spot under the big oak tree. "Maureen!" the girls cried out as they ran toward her.

"You know about the poltergeist, don't you?" Kerry launched right in.

"Yes," Maureen said flatly.

"Our Mom won't believe us," Stephanie said. "She thinks we're doing everything."

Maureen smiled her chilling smile again. In her eager-

32

ness to have the poltergeist explained, Kerry overlooked the evil in it. "Can you help us prove to our mom that a poltergeist is causing all this?"

"Come on," Maureen said, coldly. "I'll show you. And it's not *a* poltergeist."

"If it's not a poltergeist, then who . . . or *what* is it?" Kerry probed as Maureen led the girls to the back of the house.

Ignoring Kerry's question, the mysterious girl stopped near a basement window and pushed on one corner. "Watch," she said. Almost instantly, a secret door popped open.

"A secret passageway!" Stephanie and Kerry exclaimed.

Maureen nodded, flipped on a light inside the passage, then led them inside.

"I bet I know what's been going on," Stephanie said, sticking close to Maureen. "Somebody's been hiding back here and sneaking into the house and playing those pranks."

Maureen didn't bother to comment as she started to lead them up a narrow stairway.

Suddenly, warning bells started ringing in Kerry's head. This time, she heard them loud and clear and paused, suddenly afraid to follow. Maureen glanced back, saw she wasn't being followed, and stopped. "Coming, Kerry?" she asked, trying to sound innocent.

Kerry looked from her to Stephanie uncertainly. "What if we run into whoever's doing all these things?" she asked.

Impatient, Stephanie scolded her. "There are three of

us. Come on. Mom's gonna be back any minute." She turned back toward Maureen. "Go on. We're coming."

Maureen smirked as Kerry reluctantly hurried to catch up with them.

A few yards farther on, Maureen stopped and pushed open a door. Stephanie eagerly entered. Maureen stood there waiting for Kerry. Uneasy again, Kerry glanced back the way they had come.

"It's only a little farther," Maureen said.

Kerry looked at her, then hurried in after Stephanie.

The room the girls entered was completely empty. There were no windows. The only door was the one they had come through. Maureen followed them in, then closed the door. It fitted seamlessly into the wall. If Kerry didn't know there was a door there, she never would have believed it existed.

"I don't understand," Stephanie said. "There's nothing here."

"Oh, yes, there is," a girl's voice objected.

Stephanie and Kerry whirled around. There, behind them, was a duplicate of Maureen standing at an open door leading into another passageway.

"But . . . ?" Stephanie began, then stopped, not sure what to ask.

Maureen went to stand next to her duplicate.

"This is my sister, Martha," she said, then smiled a bone-chilling smile.

"We're twins, too," Martha said, then laughed because it was so obvious.

"Bye, bye," they chorused, then deftly ducked into the passageway behind them and slammed the door. It fit as seamlessly into the wall as the first one.

"Wait!" Stephanie and Kerry shouted. "Don't leave us here!" Running across the room, they began pounding on the wall. "Maureen! Martha!" they cried in unified terror.

Finally, Kerry managed to get her fear under control and stopped for a moment. "Wait, Stephanie," she said. "We're wearing ourselves out. Let's do this systematically."

"Right," Stephanie said, trying her best to mimic her sister's forced calm. She turned back toward the wall behind them. "I'll start over here," she told Kerry. "The door was here someplace." Together, the two girls began pounding the walls in an orderly fashion, desperately trying to find either the door they came through, or another way out.

Finally, Kerry tapped the wall in a certain spot and a door slid open revealing another passageway. This one was lit only by light filtering in from some faraway source and was filled with spooky shadows. "Stephanie, look!" Kerry exclaimed as she peered into the gloom.

Stephanie hurried to join Kerry at the opening. "I don't know, it's so dark," she objected.

"Would you rather stay here?" Kerry asked. Not waiting for a response, she took off her shoe. "Come on. We can wedge this in the door to keep it open and come back here if we have to."

She pulled Stephanie into the passageway, wedged her shoe in the door, and led off through the shadows. This passageway was narrower than the first and dirtier. Cobwebs brushed their hair as they passed. Creepy, furry things skittered over their feet.

"Kerry, let's go back," Stephanie whined. "This isn't going anywhere."

"Just a little bit farther," Kerry urged. "I can feel a draft. And it looks like there's a stronger light up ahead. Maybe there's a window." She rounded a corner with Stephanie right behind her.

Suddenly, both girls screamed. There, lying underneath a skylight on the floor in front of them were the skeletons of two young girls. Kerry and Stephanie stared at them in horror for a moment, then shoving, stumbling, gasping in terror, they backtracked, desperately trying to find the lighted room they had left. They searched and searched, then finally, when they were almost too weary to go another step, Kerry found the shoe she had used to prop open the door lying in the middle of the passageway. But there was no door in sight.

"No," she cried, bending over to pick it up.

Behind her, Stephanie suddenly shrank back, pointing ahead of them, scared speechless. "Kerry, look," she managed to croak.

There, hovering a few feet in front of them, were Maureen and Martha, their faces twisted in demonic grins as they floated in midair.

Kerry gasped and tried to scream, but no sound came out.

"You see," Maureen said gleefully. "It wasn't *a* poltergeist. It was *poltergeists*—with an 's.'" She grinned. "Hope you have better luck than we did getting out." A cruel laugh bubbled up from deep within her. Then, as Martha joined in, the two vanished.

Crazy with horror, the last thing Stephanie and Kerry

heard before they started mindlessly running and searching again was the disembodied voice of Maureen calling out cheerfully, "Welcome to the neighborhood!"

THE QUARTERBACK'S REVENGE

By Catherine Gourley

IT HAPPENED TWENTY years ago, but the people in Altamonte Heights still remembered. Oh, they didn't talk about it much. Mostly, they wanted to forget. It was a cold sunny Saturday in November. The team was down by a field goal. With thirty-four seconds on the clock, the Altamonte Crusaders were on their own forty-yard line. If anybody could throw a bomb, it was their quarterback, Alex Koslowski. With no time left, he took the snap and faded back, back...

The ball spiraled high. The hundreds of fans in the stadium held their breaths. Dudley leaped into the air. He caught the ball as if it was only another after-school scrimmage, not the biggest game of the year—the state playoffs. When his right foot touched down in the end zone, the fans erupted!

Suddenly, a hush replaced the roar. Koslowski was down. Ten minutes later, an ambulance crew rolled the quarterback off the field. He never regained consciousness.

After the accident, the school seriously considered for a time dropping football from its athletic program. It didn't, but the heart had gone out of the game for a lot of local people. Especially for Coach Andrew Tyler, who quit his teaching job and never coached another game.

That was twenty years ago, and time does heal. Altamonte had a new, young coach and more important, a talented quarterback—Herbie Snyder. Herbie had moved to Altamonte Heights from Michigan earlier that year and was burning up the field with his powerful arm. For the Altamonte fans, the game was fun and exciting again. Herbie Snyder took the Crusaders all the way to the state playoffs.

"I can't tell you how important this game is for me," Coach John Tyler told his players in the locker room, four days before they would play Mill Springs for the state title. "I want to win this game for my dad. Some of you may not know it, but he coached at this school twenty years ago when—" Coach Tyler hesitated. *Why bring up bad memories?* "The point is, men," he continued, "this is more than just a game. The door right now is open for every one of you."

"What door is that, Coach?" Herbie asked, grinning. He was enjoying his hero's status.

"The door to a lot of colleges and universities," said Coach. "You've gone the distance, boys. After Saturday, some of you just may walk away with scholarships."

"Do you think the scouts for Notre Dame are going to be there, Coach?" Herbie asked. "I don't want to play for anybody but Notre Dame."

The others laughed. Coach Tyler allowed himself to crack a smile, too. "Don't get cocky on me, Snyder." Then his smile faded. "I don't want anything to go wrong on Saturday."

Herbie laughed. "Hey, what could go wrong?"

Later, in the locker room as Herbie was getting dressed, Todd, the second-string quarterback, slapped Herbie playfully on the shoulder. "You know what coach was getting at, don't you?"

"Sure. We all may be fighting for the Irish next year."

"Not that. The part about his dad."

Herbie shrugged.

"I forgot," Todd said, "you're not from around here. So you don't know about the quarterback jinx."

Herbie slammed his locker door closed. "Todd, my man, I don't believe in superstitions, so quit goofing on me."

"I'm not making it up. It happened twenty years ago, the last time Altamonte was in the state playoffs. It was an accident and all, but it was pretty scary."

Herbie glanced at the clock. Karen would be waiting for him outside, but Todd had him hooked. "Okay, so tell. What happened that was *sooo* scary?"

"Well, Coach's dad was calling the shots then. The quarterback was this kid named Alex Koslowski. In the final seconds, Koslowski took a really bad hit."

Herbie felt a shiver slide up his spine. "So?" He tried to sound cool.

"So, the guy didn't make it."

"You mean—?"

Todd nodded grimly. "My dad was playing on the team. He and Alex were best friends. They were both big Miami fans."

"You mean the Hurricanes?"

Todd nodded. "Seems Alex had even heard from a Miami scout. He wanted to play for them, only he never

41

got the chance."

Herbie knew that every ball player got scared sometimes. The best learned how to control their fears, Coach Tyler had told him. Herbie shook his head, clearing away the worry that had begun to cloud his mind. He picked up his gym bag. "That's a sad story, Todd, but it's not going to happen to me. This is my game, not Alex Koslowski's."

"Yeah," Todd said, brightening a little. "The door's open for you, right?"

"Wide open, Todd," Herbie said confidently. "Wide open."

The next night after practice, Herbie found a folded piece of paper taped to the inside of his locker door. "Oooo," Tony said, walking past, "another love note from Karen?"

Herbie laughed as he unfolded the note. He stared at it a moment, then turned to Todd. "Is this your idea of a joke?" Todd took the paper and read, *My game—not yours.* "What do you think it means?"

"Why don't you tell me?"

"What—you think I wrote this?" Todd said, defensively.

"No one else was in the locker room last night when we were talking," Herbie fired back. "No one else heard me say that."

Todd straightened. "Look, I didn't write that note. Why would I?"

Herbie stared hard at Todd. He had no idea why Todd would try to psych him out before the biggest game of their lives, unless Todd was tired of playing second string. Herbie crumpled the note in his fist and walked away.

On Wednesday, Herbie's football jersey was missing. "It was here before we went on the field," he said, eyeing Todd suspiciously.

"This is too weird," Todd said.

"It's not weird," Herbie said angrily. "You're messing with my stuff, and if you don't cut it out, I'm gonna tell Coach you're sabotaging the game."

The other guys in the locker room stopped talking and turned to look at Herbie and Todd. The two quarterbacks were glaring at each other. "C'mon, you two. Knock it off," Tony said. "Save it for the game on Saturday."

Todd backed away. "You're losing it, man," he said, shaking his head.

That night with Karen, Herbie admitted he was nervous. "I'm not scared," he was quick to point out. "Just, you know, nervous."

"Why wouldn't you be?" Karen said. "There's a lot of pressure on you."

"That's right, there is." Herbie sighed. They were standing outside Karen's house, but Herbie had asked her to stay with him a few minutes longer. Karen always knew how to make him feel better about things. She reached for his left hand and turned it palm up.

"Let's see," she teased, tracing a fingertip over his smooth palm. "Oh, yes. I can see it very clearly. You are definitely going to win the game and get a scholarship to—"

He grinned. "To where?"

"—the community college right here in Altamonte Heights!"

He snatched his hand away. "No way."

She laughed. "Just kidding. Look, I've got an algebra test tomorrow. Are you okay now?"

He nodded. "Yeah, thanks for listening."

"Todd's just jealous. If anything happened to you, he'd get to play in the big game."

"Todd wouldn't jeopardize the game just so he could play," Herbie said. But the truth was, Herbie wasn't so sure about that.

That night, he tossed in his sleep. After midnight, he bolted out of bed and stood in the middle of his room in the dark, eyes searching for the voice that had whispered in his ear, *My game . . . my life.* No one was there. He rubbed his eyes. "Just a bad dream," he muttered. "Just a bad dream."

THE NEXT AFTERNOON, Coach worked the team hard during practice. Afterward, as the others trotted back to the locker room, he called Herbie aside. "What's up, Herbie? You were distracted out there."

Herbie shrugged. "I'm okay, Coach. I just didn't sleep too well. Thinking about the game and all." He repeated what Karen had told him last night. "There's a lot of pressure on me. A lot of people are counting on me to win this thing."

Coach raised an eyebrow. "Listen up, Herbie. There's no 'I' in team. There are ten other players on that field working with you to make this victory happen. Don't you forget that."

"Yes, sir."

Then the coach relented. He tapped Herbie on the

side of the head. "You've got what it takes, kid. You're going to do fine out there on Saturday. Now go home and get some sleep."

Herbie was late getting to the locker room. The others were already dressed and leaving. His right shoulder was sore, and he stayed a long time in the shower, letting the hot water work out the kinks. When he finally turned off the water and stepped out of the shower, the locker room was empty. Standing in front of the steamy mirrors, he began to towel his hair dry. Then he heard it, a soft sound like leaves rustling.

"*My game.*"

Herbie froze, the towel in his hands.

"*My life.*" It was a low whisper.

"Todd!" Herbie shouted, whirling around. No one was there. Water dripped from the shower heads. Locker doors hung open. But the room was deserted. "Coach?" Herbie called out. No answer. Herbie was alone.

When he looked in the mirror again, he caught his breath. Two faces were staring back at him through the steamy glass—his and another's. The boy was about Herbie's age, but Herbie had never seen him before. "*My life,*" the face said.

"No!" Herbie roared. When he wiped the steam from the mirror with his towel, the face disappeared.

Karen was waiting outside. Everyone else was gone and Herbie had still not come out. She paced. It was dark, and she was worried. Finally, the gymnasium door opened and Herbie hurried out, his football jacket unbuttoned. His face was white. What he told her was too incredible.

"Are you sure you didn't imagine it?" she asked.

"I saw him," Herbie repeated. "He had curly brown hair. Kind of long and shaggy against his neck. He was taller than me. I saw him, Karen. I did."

"Okay, okay. I believe you saw . . ." she hesitated. "Someone."

"No, I saw *him*. Koslowski. The quarterback."

"Herbie, listen to me." Karen spoke softly. "Alex Koslowski died twenty years ago."

"All I know is what I saw. And heard."

Karen sighed. "Let me prove it to you. Come with me."

"Where?"

"Just come," she insisted.

KAREN HANDED HER request to the research librarian. "Can we see this on microfilm?"

The librarian read the date Karen had scribbled on the piece of paper. "Twenty years ago? Yes, we have this in the back room."

A moment later, the librarian returned with the box of microfilm. Karen led Herbie to a large machine at the rear of the building where she threaded the film over the wheels. As the tape whizzed through the machine, time spun backwards. Days and weeks ticked off in seconds. "Here," Karen said, stopping the machine and focusing on the headline of the *Altamonte Heights Courier.* "Oh no!" she gasped.

"It's him!" Herbie cried.

The boy with the dark, curly hair was staring at them from the screen. His eyes were dark and determined. But what had startled Karen was the headline on Alex

Koslowski's obituary: *His Game, His Life.*

"That's what you heard, isn't it?" she asked, unable to tear her eyes from the screen.

Herbie nodded. He could not speak.

A second picture of Alex showed him in uniform, right arm cocked, ready to throw the ball, left arm extended palm up toward the camera as if blocking a tackle. "Look. He had a scar on his left palm," said Karen.

Herbie flipped the light off on the machine and the image of Alex Koslowski faded into darkness. "Okay," he said, his voice no longer wavering and frightened. "So Koslowski is dead. Now I know that what I saw tonight really was just my imagination." He shook his head, smiling. "Crazy stuff, huh? Stress and all that. Let's get out of here."

"But you described him just the way he looked—" Karen protested.

Herbie shrugged. "Coincidence. Curly hair, tall—that could describe anybody."

"Those eyes," she said and shuddered. "They were so piercing, as if he really was looking out at us from the machine."

Herbie laughed at her. "No one believes in ghosts, Karen."

Karen said nothing. She rewound the film and returned it to the librarian. They walked home in silence. But before going into her house, Karen looked into Herbie's eyes and begged him not to play on Saturday.

"What? I have to. And I want to. This is the game of my life!"

"Please," she said. "I'm scared."

"Look, Karen, how would it sound if I went to Coach and said, 'I had a dream about this Koslowski dude and I'm not going to play today.' Or better yet, I could tell him his ghost appeared to me in the locker room. Right. Coach would think I was nuts."

"Then just say you're sick."

"Karen, I can always count on you to help me. You took me to the library and showed me the proof: Koslowski is dead."

SATURDAY WAS COLD, but sunny. Through three quarters, Herbie struggled to get the Crusaders on the scoreboard. He couldn't seem to connect on his long passes, and the other team sacked him eight times. By the fourth quarter, the score was Mill Springs 6, Altamonte Heights 0. Herbie was bruised sore from the beating he had taken. The Crusaders were on their own forty with less than a minute left on the clock. In the huddle, Herbie called the play. "Go long, Tony," he said. "Just get down there."

"I'll be there," said Tony. "Just hit me this time."

The huddle broke. The center snapped the ball. Herbie faded back, back...

Then Herbie heard, like a tiny voice inside his helmet. *My game...*

A Mill Springs guard broke through the line and dove for Herbie.

My life...

Herbie got the ball off. The pigskin spiraled high in the air. Tony leaped, caught it, and touched it down in the end zone. The fans went wild.

But suddenly, their cheers stopped. Herbie Snyder was down and very still. In the stands, Karen screamed. She pushed her way out of the bleachers and rushed down the concrete stadium steps. A security officer stopped her at the gate to the field. "Sorry, miss," he said.

"You don't understand. He's my boyfriend!"

On the field, Herbie opened his eyes. He saw the face of the tall, curly-haired boy leaning over him. "Don't move," Koslowski said. "Everything is going to be all right."

"No," Herbie murmured. Then everything went dark.

"HE'S A LUCKY boy," the doctor said later that night. "Only a concussion. We'll keep him in the hospital until tomorrow to make sure, but I'm positive he's going to be good as new."

Herbie's parents smiled in relief. They squeezed Karen's shoulder. "Can I see him now?" she asked.

Herbie's mother smiled. "Sure. We'll wait out here."

Karen opened the door. Herbie was lying in the hospital bed. He smiled when he saw her. "Oh, Herbie," she cried. "I was *so* scared!" She stood beside his bed.

"I guess I really am a football hero now," he said. "I won the game, didn't I?"

"You sure did." She beamed. "Are you sure you're all right?"

"Just a couple of black eyes, that's all." He smiled. "But I feel like I've been asleep for years." He held out his left hand to her. "Come closer, Karen."

As she reached for his hand, she noticed a long white scar across his palm. It hadn't been there yesterday.

"Did you get that—" She stared at Herbie, unable to finish her sentence.

"What?" he said. "Oh, that? I fell off my bike when I was a kid. You know that hill on Pine Street?"

"Pine Street? You mean, right here in Altamonte Heights?"

"Yeah. I cut my hand real bad."

Karen frowned. "But Herbie, I thought you grew up in Michigan."

"Oh," he said. "Yeah. Guess I'm mixed up. Banged on the head and all." He winked.

Karen couldn't remember Herbie's ever winking at her. He said guys looked nerdy when they tried to impress girls by winking at them.

"Why are you staring at me like that?" Herbie asked.

There was something different about him. She wasn't sure what it was. His face was bruised and the skin around his eyes swollen and dark, but it wasn't that. It was the way he was looking at her. "Your eyes," she began.

Then the door opened and Todd, Tony, and a few other guys from the team piled into the room, crowding around Herbie's bed. "Hey, Mr. Quarterback, Mr. State Champion," they laughed. "Didn't Notre Dame send you any flowers?"

Herbie made a face. "Why would I want flowers from Notre Dame? Now maybe a basket of oranges from the Hurricanes, that would be nice."

Karen looked at him quickly. Notre Dame was Herbie's favorite team.

"You were out cold, man," Todd said. "You had us all scared."

"Yeah," said Herbie seriously. "It's great to be back among the living."

Karen felt as if the breath were being squeezed out of her. She dropped Herbie's hand and stepped back. The scar...the scar hadn't been there yesterday. She was sure of it.

Herbie leaned forward and took her wrist. "Where are you going, Karen?"

His eyes . . . they were dark and staring hard at her. They were not Herbie's eyes. Karen smiled weakly. "I thought maybe you'd want to talk to the guys a while— you know, alone."

But his fingers tightened around her arm. "Don't go, Karen."

"I have to." She tried to pull away from him. "Let me go."

"No," he said. "Stay." He pulled her toward him, his eyes staring deep into hers. With his mouth so close she could feel his cold breath against her ear, he whispered, "What are you afraid of, Karen? No one believes in ghosts."

BEAT BART

By Robert C. Welch

OLIVER DROPPED HIS book bag on the floor and plopped down onto his desk chair. He switched on his computer, punched the power button for the monitor, and waited while the hard drive checked itself for errors. After a moment the computer beeped the "all-clear" and the monitor displayed a simulated desktop.

He slid the mouse until it was centered over the tiny telephone symbol and clicked the button. In seconds he was in his communication software. He scrolled through the numbers in his phone book and selected the number for GameTime, a bulletin board he had recently discovered that catered especially to computer gamers.

When he was prompted, he entered his identification number and password. Then the standard greeting was displayed on the screen and the server waited for his response.

"Okay," Oliver said out loud, a habit he had developed while he was using the networks. "What's it going to be today?"

He decided to look in the section titled New Stuff. Posted there was an announcement for a brand-new interactive game which loudly claimed that it was BETTER THAN VIRTUAL REALITY!

"I doubt that," Oliver scoffed. But he called up the announcement on his screen anyway to see what it had to say for itself.

"BEAT BART," the announcement read. "The new generation of computer gaming. You've all experienced the hokey graphics and jerky movements of most other computer games. BEAT BART is as far advanced from these clunkers as your computer is from a calculator. BEAT BART combines the newest advances in virtual reality programming with the high degree of personal involvement you get from interactive games. When you play BEAT BART you're not just playing a computer simulation, you're playing against other people! Both of you in a computer-simulated setting that's so real you'll have trouble remembering it's 'only a game.'"

"BEAT BART will be brought on-line in over 100 different cities over the next month. BEAT BART is compatible with most joysticks, or you can order the BARTGUN from our on-line order number. If you try only one new game this year, make it BEAT BART. You'll never want to play another."

Oliver read through the list of dates that followed. "Excellent!" he yelled. His was one of the cities that would be part of the BEAT BART start-up. Marking the date on his desk calendar, Oliver moved on to the order line to buy the BARTGUN.

As the demonstration date drew closer, Oliver became nearly sleepless with excitement. His best friend, Rob, had moved the summer before to the east coast. Now Rob lived in one of the cities where BEAT BART had made its first appearance. The day after Rob tried it he called Oliver.

"It's fantastic!" Rob promised. "You're not going to believe it."

"How does it work?" Oliver demanded.

"It's really cool. But you gotta order the gun."

"I did." He didn't tell his friend that his parents had almost refused to let him buy it, even though he had the money saved up from his allowance. His dad thought there were enough kids getting killed by real guns without having games that centered around gunplay. It had been a tough fight, but after Oliver had promised to mow the lawn without ever complaining again, his dad gave in.

"The gun is what makes it happen," Rob went on enthusiastically. "You gotta use it to shoot and to *see*."

"What do you mean, see?"

"Well, it's a bit weird at first, but you point the gun in whatever direction you want to look and what you're seeing shows up on your screen."

"Kind of like a mouse."

"Yeah. But a hundred times faster. No joke, you just flick your wrist and the screen changes—it's that fast. Takes a little getting used to."

"Is that how you move, too?"

"Nope. For that, you need your mouse. That was kind of tough, too—using it with my left hand."

"Then what happens?"

"You pick whatever setting you want—I think there's Old West, Big City, Futuristic, and a couple of others. I picked Old West, and it starts you off on the outskirts of a town. The whole point is to find and shoot the other guy before he shoots you. But the best part is that the other guys are other players."

"What?"

"Yeah! Somewhere there's someone else logged on and they're looking for you. That's what makes it so cool. You can play a hundred times and have a hundred different enemies."

"Is it tough?" Oliver asked.

"Not really," Rob said. "The guy I was going against didn't have a clue. I nailed him in the first five minutes. Then I played a couple more with some guys who were better, but I still won. I'm working my way up to Bart."

"Who's that?"

"Bart is the computer, or probably the programmer. Anyway, after you have a certain number of kills you go up against Bart."

After talking to Rob, Oliver could hardly wait for his own chance to BEAT BART. Finally, the day arrived, and Oliver raced straight home from school. He wanted to get logged on fast in case there were a limited number of open ports. He waited impatiently for his computer to boot, then dialed the BEAT BART phone number.

"Welcome to BEAT BART," the screen flashed in bright red colors. "If you have bought a BARTGUN, please enter the serial number now."

Oliver did so, and stared at the screen.

"Hello, Oliver. Are you ready to try your luck?"

"YES," Oliver typed.

"Good. Please connect your BARTGUN if you have not already done so. Then download the file BART.EXE to your computer. It will require 275k of memory. When you are done, point the gun at the center of your screen and follow the on-screen instructions."

Oliver did as instructed and once the program was in, he pointed the gun at the screen. Then he followed a set of exercises designed both to initiate his computer and to give him some practice on how to use the gun. Rob was right—it did take getting used to. Oliver had to keep reminding himself that "forward" was the direction his gun was pointing, so that he actually turned with the gun and not the mouse.

When he was finished practicing, the computer asked him to choose his setting. Smiling, he took aim at "Old West" and pulled the trigger.

"Please enter the name you would like to be known as, or type [Enter] for your own name."

Oliver thought a moment, then typed "MAD DOG."

"Okay, MAD DOG. Do you have a specific challenge in mind? Or are you open to all comers?"

The only other person Oliver knew was Rob, and he didn't know Rob's game name. He typed "OPEN."

His screen displayed a weathered signboard with the message, "You've just been informed that LEE THE KID has been seen riding for town. Last time you saw him he said you'd better be gone when he next came through town or he'd come hunting for you. The townspeople won't get involved, but they wish you luck." The sign-board disappeared, and his screen showed an elevated view of an old western town.

Oliver stared at the monitor in surprise. The picture was so clear and crisp it seemed as if he was staring out a window. The only odd part was the crosshairs of the gunsight floating in midair. The hand holding his gun dropped to the desk.

Suddenly, the view tilted crazily and settled on a view of two feet in cowboy boots standing on dry, brown soil. With a disbelieving smile, Oliver slowly raised his hand and pointed the gun straight ahead. The view righted itself.

"All right," Oliver drawled in an excited whisper.

One hand resting gently on his mouse and the BART-GUN in his other, Mad Dog walked into town to face Lee the Kid.

BY THE TIME his mother called him for dinner, Oliver was a seasoned veteran of three gunfights. Contrary to what Rob had told him, he had come up against a pretty good player on his first outing. It was only through sheer luck that he had managed to win.

He had been walking through town, amazed at the way the screen changed perspective with such fluid ease. With a little imagination he really could believe he was walking down the dusty street of a western town. No matter where he pointed his gun there was something on the screen, even when he looked behind him. And there were people, too! The town was fully populated with men, women, and children who watched him solemnly as he gawked his way down Main Street. Some of them called out a greeting, which he heard through his computer speaker. "I'll have to get a sound board," Oliver noted to himself.

His sightseeing saved him in his first shoot-out. He had just passed a general store when he suddenly decided

to see if the computer would allow him to enter it. He slid the mouse to take a quick step backwards. At that moment he heard the crack of a gunshot, and a chip of wood blasted away from the post next to his head.

Oliver jumped, and the monitor showed buildings, sky, and earth swirling madly as his hand waved the gun around. Meanwhile, his reaction had slid the mouse all the way to one side, sending him flying backwards through the doorway of the store.

There was another shot and the glass pane in the door shattered. Oliver managed to get his gun pointed out the window so he could look around.

Across the street was a man in dirty brown clothes. He was standing behind a post, sighting down his gun barrel at the door of the store. Without pausing to see if the man was in his sights, Oliver squeezed the trigger. There was a bang and to his shock he saw the man stagger out from behind the post.

Oliver had hit him in the shoulder and blood was soaking the man's shirt. He staggered forward, bringing up his gun to point it at Oliver. This time Oliver centered the crosshairs on the man's chest when he pulled the trigger. With a spray of blood, the man flew backwards to lie motionless in the street.

Suddenly, Oliver was back outside of town, facing the weathered signboard.

"Congratulations, MAD DOG. By ridding us all of scum like LEE THE KID you have made Bartville a safer place to live. You have one notch in your gun grip. Care to try for another?"

The next battle had lasted much longer, as both

Oliver and his opponent spent most of their time sneaking around town taking shots at each other, rather than forcing an outright duel. Finally, Oliver shot the other from a second-floor window.

The third battle was much the same, but this time Oliver tried running as fast as he could to the other side of town to get the drop on his man. It seemed to work—the enemy wasn't even paying attention when he walked by Oliver's hiding place.

Over the next few weeks Oliver played BEAT BART as often as he could. He told all his friends at school about the game, but only one of them, Randy, had the required hardware. Oliver's parents were a little worried about his "obsession" with the game, but he was on his best behavior otherwise, so they let him continue.

Oliver called Rob sometimes to compare notes, but they made a promise never to tell each other their Western names. "You'll know me when you fight me, though," said Rob. "I have a neat little trick that wins me about half the battles I'm in." He refused to tell Oliver any more than that.

They began an informal contest to see who could earn the most notches on his gun grip. As each of them survived more and more battles, they raced neck and neck to the ultimate goal—to play against and beat Bart himself.

One day Randy swaggered theatrically up to Oliver on the playground. "You varmint," he said in his best imitation of a Wild West gunslinger, "I'm calling you out!"

Oliver answered with a fierce scowl. "Name the time, you fleabitten dog."

"Tonight. Eight o'clock. If you ain't yellow."

"I'll be there," Oliver nodded. "What's your name, stranger? So's I can get it right on your tombstone."

"Folks call me 'Killer.'"

"Well, Killer, you've just run up against Mad Dog. And tonight at eight, you're gonna get bit!"

That was too much for Randy, and he burst out laughing. Oliver dropped his mean look and joined in.

"So how do we do this?" Randy asked.

"I'm not sure. I guess when you log on, you specify that you want a challenge. When it asks for a name, type Mad Dog."

"Got it, Mad Dog. I'll be waiting on-line at eight o'clock."

"See you in Bartville," Oliver agreed.

It wasn't until Oliver logged on that night that he realized how close he was to having enough notches to challenge Bart. By pure chance, winning this battle against Randy would put him in the eligible column. "If you do," he reminded himself grimly.

The signboard informed him that a challenge had been issued by KILLER, and asked if he wanted to accept it. Excited and nervous, Oliver entered "YES."

It seemed like ages before he logged off. Randy had been good—real good. For a time Oliver had really been worried that he wouldn't be able to beat his friend. Bad enough that he would have had to start over on the path to Bart. But to have to face Randy the next day would have been unbearable.

Oliver sat back and felt his sweat-drenched shirt against his skin. The long battle had ended pretty spectacularly. He had aimed and fired in one motion, and had managed to hit Killer smack in the gun hand. With a vivid spray of blood his right hand had been ruined. When Randy tried to run, Oliver chased after him and plugged him in the back as he was sprinting down the street.

Of course, Oliver would never ever admit to Randy that his first shot had been pure luck—he had really been aiming for Killer's chest!

The next day at school he waited out front for the ex-Killer, but Randy didn't show up. He wasn't at lunch, either, and Oliver began to suspect he was so embarrassed he had skipped school.

"He's not going to get away with that," Oliver promised himself. After school he rode over to Randy's house. He rang the doorbell and stood on the porch flashing a big, triumphant grin.

Randy's father opened the door. He looked awful, pale with dark circles under his eyes. His clothes were all wrinkled, as if he had slept in them, but he didn't look as if he had slept at all.

"Uh, hi, Mister Reese," Oliver said. "Is Randy home?"

Mr. Reese looked at Oliver for a long moment, as if he were trying to place the familiar face. Then he said slowly, "Oliver. Randy was killed last night."

Oliver's eyes bugged out. He felt like his jaw was about to hit his knees. "What? How? I mean...I'm sorry but, well...Mister Reese, how did it happen?"

Randy's father answered in a voice as dead as his son. "We don't know. We found him this morning in his bedroom, shot."

A small, cold hand seemed to run its fingers along Oliver's spine. "Shot?" he squeaked.

"That's right," Mr. Reese said in his dull voice. "Right in his own room. We didn't hear a thing, but we found him there this morning."

Oliver gulped and shook his head a little to clear his ears. Even as he asked the next question, he told himself that what he was thinking just wasn't possible.

"Where—where was he shot?" he asked in a small voice.

Mr. Reese's mouth stretched in a ghastly imitation of a smile. "That's the strange part, you know? He was shot twice. Once in the hand and once, according to the police doctor, in the back."

Oliver mumbled something and stumbled away from the door. He groped blindly for his bike and turned for home.

"It's just not possible!" he told himself. "It must be some sort of crazy coincidence!" But what kind of coincidence could explain a thirteen-year-old kid being shot for no reason, in the middle of his room, in exactly the same places Oliver had shot him in a computer game the night before?

He stopped pedaling and coasted to a stop in front of his house. If what he was thinking were true, then what about all those other people he had killed while playing BEAT BART? Even worse, what about all the other people who were playing? Shivers racked his body as his mind began to add up the numbers. Randy's death had to be a coincidence. It had to be.

Oliver made his way to the phone and called Rob. There was no answer, even though it was later in the evening on Rob's end. He hung up and went to his room.

He found himself staring at the BEAT BART sign-board. He had no memory of sitting down and logging on, but the suddenly eerie signboard was there on his screen.

"Congratulations, MAD DOG," the signboard read. "You are now eligible to challenge BART for the title of Master Gunslinger. Do you wish to challenge BART now?"

Oliver stared at the screen so long his screen saver winked on. If it were just a game, then he was acting like an idiot. But if, somehow, it were not he might be risking his life. Thoughts swirling, he deliberately aimed and shot out the word "YES." He had to try to kill Bart—to save all the others who were playing this horrible game.

Like all the others, the game began with Oliver on the outskirts of town. More cautious than ever, he carefully made his way into Bartville.

Long before, Oliver had discovered that you didn't have to approach town in a direct line from where you began. His usual practice was to circle around to the opposite side of town. Sometimes, when he was lucky, he could come up behind the other player and the battle would be over before it had even begun.

This time, however, something occurred that had never happened before. As he was making his way in a large circuit around Bartville, he saw another man doing the same! Moving quickly, Oliver jumped down into a gully and raced in the opposite direction.

Bart was good! he thought frantically. And if he was too good, what did that mean for Oliver?

Time passed without meaning as Oliver and Bart

moved in an intricate dance through and around Bartville. Every now and then one would catch a glimpse of the other, and shots would crack over the speaker. But neither fighter was able to get a bead on his opponent.

Then, on as simple a thing as turning a corner a second before the other gunman, the match was over. Oliver's bullet took Bart just to the right of the middle of his chest. The other gunman seemed to get drawn up onto his toes, where he balanced for an instant before slowly toppling over like a cut tree.

Wearily, Oliver let his gun slump down, and the screen obligingly showed him the dirt at his feet. After a moment, he realized how odd that was. At the end of every other battle he had been instantly presented with the signboard on the outskirts of town. This time, he remained standing in the street.

Raising his gun, he looked around. A crowd was cautiously gathering in a rough oval around him and the fallen Bart. Suddenly curious to see what face the computer gave itself, Oliver walked over to the dead body.

His breath caught in his throat and he gasped. "No!" Lying in a patch of bloody mud was Rob. His eyes stared upwards and he blinked when Oliver came into his field of vision.

"Congratulations, Bart," he whispered. Then his eyes slowly rolled back in his head.

"That's right, son," said the old man who was standing next to Oliver. He clapped a friendly hand on Oliver's arm and *Oliver felt it.* "Now you're the Master Gunslinger. Glad to have you with us."

Oliver could smell the dusty air and feel the warm sun

on his back. He could hear the townspeople murmuring. The old man looked down at Rob's lifeless body, then back up at Oliver. "Sure hope you last longer than that one did."

WHAT GOES AROUND COMES AROUND

By Anne Bancroft Fowler

WHAT GOES AROUND, comes around," Dillon had said just before he died. Jennifer bit her lip at the memory. His funeral had been last November, four months ago, but his words still came back to haunt her.

She knew that what she had done was wrong, but she'd wanted so badly to win the competition. She *had* to win.

It had all started innocently enough, in the computer lab at school....

―――――――――

JENNIFER'S LAPTOP COMPUTER was in for repairs. The deadline for the writing contest was the next day, so she went to the computer lab to put the finishing touches on her entry.

There was already a disk in the drive of the computer she chose, but the screen had gone back to the main menu. She reached to exchange the disk for her own, but on a sudden impulse decided to sneak a peek at what was on the disk instead.

A story came up on the screen. It was about a boy from a poor neighborhood. He was a member of a motorcycle gang, and his secret ambition was to write. From the moment she began to read, Jennifer knew the story would win the contest. It was real life, written with an intensity she had never been able to achieve in her own writing.

She glanced around. No one was watching. Without hesitation, she popped the disk out of the computer and put it in her purse. Dillon came in just as Jennifer was leaving.

"Hey!" she heard him say as she walked out the door. "What happened to the disk I was working on?"

Jennifer ignored him, and hurried off.

"Jennifer, wait!" Dillon called after her. "I need to ask you something!"

Jennifer pretended not to hear him. "See you tomorrow, Dillon!" she called. Outside, she unlocked her bike and peeled out of the school lot. *What am I doing?* Jennifer thought, as she sped along the tree-lined streets toward her home. *I must be crazy to think I can get away with something like this. Dillon is bound to have other copies of his work.*

Then, suddenly, she heard the grinding of metal as someone rode up beside her. It was Dillon. How had he caught up to her on his crummy old one-speed bike?

"Wait up," he said breathlessly, his face red from pedaling hard. "I want to talk to you."

Jennifer ignored him. Eyes straight ahead, she downshifted a gear on her sleek, twenty-one-speed bike and shot ahead. But Dillon wasn't giving up. Within seconds he pulled up alongside her once more. "This won't do you any good!" he shouted.

Jennifer turned to look at him. They locked angry stares. Then Dillon looked back at the road ahead just in time for him to see a toddler chase a ball into the street.

"Look out!" he shouted. Jennifer looked and froze. Dillon reached over and grabbed her handlebar to steer her away from the child. As he did, he lost control of his own bike, hit the curb, flipped, and came down hard. He was thrown twenty yards, and his unfastened helmet was torn away on impact.

Jennifer's bike hit a tree down the street across from the toddler, who watched the twin crashes with mild interest from midstreet, the ball safely in his hands.

Someone cried out and ran to call the paramedics. A crowd began to gather. Dazedly, Jennifer tried to pull herself away from her mangled bike. "Stay where you are," someone told her.

"Dillon?" She looked around.

His body lay stretched out on the grass nearby. His eyes were open, focused on her. His voice was faint, but distinct. "What goes around, comes around," he said, and then he smiled with a funny little twist of his lips.

Jennifer didn't know if he died then or on the way to the hospital. She was all right, herself. A few bruises and a sore elbow were all she had to show for the accident.

"I saw the whole thing," said a heavyset man, getting out of his car. "The boy was chasing her," he told the gathering crowd, pointing to Jennifer. "He was yelling at her to wait, then he grabbed her handlebar and tried to make her stop."

Jennifer was sent to the hospital and held overnight for observation. She told the police who came to take her statement that she couldn't remember exactly what happened. "No," she said in answer to their questioning.

"I don't know why he was chasing me."

The school delayed the writing competition deadline five days, until after Dillon's funeral. That was enough time for Jennifer to make Dillon's story over into her own. She attended the funeral with a long face, but a few hours later was sitting in front of her computer, copying Dillon's disk onto her hard drive. Then she hid the disk in a shoe box at the back of her closet.

Just as she knew it would, the story won the school competition, then went on to win at the state level. And although Jennifer's English teacher was surprised at the sudden forcefulness of her style, no one questioned the straight-A student.

Almost no one.

It was during Christmas vacation that Jennifer began to see Dillon out of the corner of her eye. In the mall, or at the skating rink, there he was, watching her from a distance. He always wore a twisted smile, and he was always gone when she turned to look him full in the face.

The first phone call came in January, after Jennifer's story won the national competition and was printed in the local paper. "What goes around, comes around," came the whispered words. It was Dillon's voice. Then there was only a dial tone. Jennifer took the phone off the hook, then closed all the drapes until her parents came home from work.

THE NEXT WEEK at school, Jennifer saw Dillon standing in the doorway at the end of the hall. She recognized his slouching walk, his leather jacket, and that horrible gash he'd gotten on his forehead from the accident.

"Look!" she said, clutching her friend Merilee's arm and pointing. But as suddenly as he had appeared, Dillon was gone.

"Look at what?" Merilee asked, running after Jennifer, who had reached the end of the hall and was looking wildly around the empty schoolyard.

"Didn't you see him?" Jennifer asked Merilee, her voice shaking.

"See who? There's nobody here. What's the matter with you lately?"

"You wouldn't understand," Jennifer snapped.

"Well, pardon me, your highness." Merilee moved off, muttering, "Winning contests sure changes some people."

From that time on, Jennifer began to watch for Dillon in earnest. She saw him once in the market and once in the movie theater, but he always disappeared before she could get too close.

On Valentine's Day everyone in the class got a special valentine...everyone except Jennifer.

She heard about it from Merilee. "This was in my locker. Everybody's asking me what it means." She gave Jennifer a piece of paper the color of blood.

It was written like a poem. Jennifer read:

Our Jennifer would like to hide
the secret we have found,
but she's afraid because she knows
the truth will come around.

Beneath the poem was printed in crude block letters: "WHAT GOES AROUND COMES AROUND."

Jennifer stopped in her tracks in the center of the busy hall. Students pushed around her, rushing to class. She could see red sheets in their hands. Several turned to look at her. The blood drained from her face, and her knees felt ready to give way. Jennifer looked around. A group of girls was watching her.

Merilee took her aside. "Look, Jen. This is getting too weird. You have to tell me what's going on."

With an effort, Jennifer pulled herself together. "Nothing's going on. It's just somebody's idea of a joke." She turned and walked away, leaving Merilee staring after her, frowning.

Jennifer went straight to the nurse's office and asked to go home, pleading illness. She was, in fact, sick with fear, and her ashen face convinced the nurse. *How could they know?* she kept thinking, over and over again.

At home, she tore up the stairs and into her closet, throwing boxes aside until she found the one with Dillon's disk. She checked to make sure the disk was still there, then she put the box at the back of her closet behind everything that would fit in front of it.

Her mother came home from work to find Jennifer in bed with the lights out. "What's wrong, Jenny?" she asked. "Are you sick?"

"No, Mom. I just need some time alone." It had been their custom ever since Jennifer had been a little girl to talk over any problems she had, but this was one problem Jennifer couldn't tell anyone.

Jennifer turned her back and pulled the pillow over her head.

The next day, Jennifer actually had a slight fever, so

her mother let her stay home. Then it was the weekend, and she stayed in bed almost the whole time. On Monday, though, her mother insisted she go back to school. Luckily, by then the valentine letters had disappeared. Jennifer was able to pass it off as a practical joke, but her anxiety remained. She dreaded what would come next.

"The editor of the school yearbook wants you to write a story," her English teacher told her on Friday. "Along the lines of the one you wrote for the competition. It's a great honor to be asked to write for the annual, particularly since you're not a senior."

"Me?" Jennifer asked. The word came out like a strangled croak.

"I told them you would," the teacher said, smiling.

"You shouldn't have done that!" Jennifer blurted. Then seeing the puzzled look the teacher gave her, she added, "I mean, I haven't been writing lately."

"I know. All the more reason for you to get back in gear. Consider it an English assignment."

"But…"

"I don't want to argue about this, Jennifer. I'll expect something by Monday."

At home later, Jennifer sat down at her computer and tried to write, but the words wouldn't come. She knew she couldn't write something like the winning entry. She might never be able to write anything again.

As she sat there, staring at the blank screen, her mother called to say she would be late and to please start dinner. "Your dad has to work late, so it'll be just the two of us," her mother said. "And by the way, there's a surprise for you in the garage."

JENNIFER SHOOK HER head and sighed as she stood in front of the brand-new bike in the garage. She picked up the card lying on the seat and read: *Cheer up, sweetheart. We love you, Mom & Dad.*

Nearly bursting into tears, Jennifer dropped the card and ran upstairs. She *had* to write something. She sat down at the computer, but once again nothing came to her. Then she had an idea.

She went to her closet, pulled out the shoe box, and retrieved Dillon's disk. She put it into the A drive and pulled the directory up on the screen. The first listing was the story she had stolen, and under that were several other documents that bore abbreviated titles she couldn't identify. Jennifer pulled one up. It was a list of colleges. She exited and tried again.

The second was somebody's homework, a history paper. She kept going. On the fifth try, she found something that looked like another story. She began to read— at first with interest, then with increasing horror.

In the story, a spoiled girl wanted to get into a certain college at any cost. She went so far as to steal a story from a classmate and enter it in a writing contest. She won, but the classmate exposed her act of plagiarism to the whole school. The girl was expelled in disgrace, and her contest prize was stripped away. The moral of the story was contained in the last line, when the hero said to her, "What goes around, comes around."

"No!" Jennifer screamed, snatching the disk from the drive and hurling it across the room. She threw herself

across the bed, sobbing wildly. As she lay there, the phone rang. Jennifer debated whether to answer it and decided not to. But the ringing went on and on, and she finally snatched up the receiver. "Hello?"

"What goes around, comes around." The voice breathed into the receiver.

"Dillon!" Jennifer cried. "Why are you doing this?" She sobbed and held the receiver away, staring at it. Then she dropped it and jumped up from the bed to search for the disk. Retrieving it from where it had fallen behind the nightstand, she fled to the garage.

Nearly flying as she sped away on her new bike, she barely missed a neighbor who was crossing the street. "Hey! Watch where you're going," he called after her as she raced off.

She knew exactly where she was going, but she was concentrating so hard on the traffic around her that she almost missed the turnoff to the cemetery. She sped through the gated entrance to the graveyard, trying to remember where Dillon's grave lay.

At last she found the grave site. It was at the top of the hill, in a section of new grass. She dropped her bike and threw herself to her knees with a sob. "I'm sorry, Dillon," she wailed. "Please forgive me." She took the disk from her coat pocket and dropped it on the ground. "Look! I've brought your disk. I'm going to give it back." She began digging at the earth with her bare hands. She was so intent on her task that she didn't hear the footsteps approaching from behind.

Suddenly, a black shadow loomed over her. She looked over her shoulder. There, his figure blocking the

setting sun behind him, was Dillon.

Jennifer jumped to her feet with a scream. Dillon took a step toward her. She started to run.

"Wait," he said. "I want to talk to you."

Jennifer ran to her bike and raced down the hillside. She thought she heard someone riding behind her, but she dared not look back.

With a pounding heart, she pumped harder, flying out the cemetery gate and onto the street. *I know this part of town*, she thought frantically. *I can lose myself in one of the back streets.* Searching for a place to turn, she saw a movement out of the corner of her eye. Turning to look, she saw Dillon coming behind her, flashing the headlight on his bike. Jennifer pedaled with all her might, and her bike responded with a spurt of speed. She made it to the end of the block and turned right.

As she looked over her shoulder, she saw that Dillon was still behind her, and still gaining. She flew around the next corner. A station wagon was double-parked in the street, with children climbing out from all doors. Jennifer hit the brakes and turned the front wheel sharply. The brakes locked, and her bike went out of control, plunging across the street right into a telephone pole. Jennifer was thrown off and landed several feet away. She heard the sound of running steps, but she felt no pain. She fought for consciousness.

She looked up into Dillon's face. He took her hand. She could feel the warmth flow from his body into hers. She tried to focus, to speak.

"Don't try to talk."

The voice was like Dillon's and yet it was not. His

image was growing fuzzy. "You're not Dillon," she said. "Who are you?"

"His cousin."

Things were growing dark now, closing in around her, but she had to know. "How did you...?"

"How did I know? I wouldn't have if the story hadn't won the contest and been published in the paper. You see, I wrote that story, not Dillon. I tried to talk to you back there at the cemetery, but you ran away."

She gave a little sigh. "What goes around..."

Her eyes closed, and Dillon's cousin moved out of the way of the paramedic, who was vainly trying to find a pulse in Jennifer's lifeless body.

THE WITCH
By Sandra K. Bailey

MELANIE OWENS IRRITABLY tore the No Trespassing sign off the fence and hid it behind a bush. Crabby old Mrs. Crandall had finally made good on her threat to put up a sign. Too bad she was the one who owned the entire four acres at the end of the cul-de-sac where Melanie lived. Crossing through her property was the only way to get from Melanie's street to the park on the other side without going all the way around the block.

How can she even see me? Melanie wondered as she climbed the fence and started making her way along a dirt path through the acreage. The whole place was so over-grown with weird plants and cluttered with junk that it seemed impossible to her that anyone could actually see someone crossing through it.

Almost there, Melanie thought, pushing an overgrown vine out of the way. *Mrs. Crandall is just being mean,* she reassured herself. *It's not like I'm hurting anything.* As she continued to press on, Melanie didn't notice that her feet were squashing one delicate plant after another.

The next day, the No Trespassing sign was hanging on the fence again. This time, Mrs. Crandall had added, "This means *you*, Melanie Owens!"

That old crab, Melanie thought. She tried to remove the sign, but Mrs. Crandall had pounded so many nails into it that an elephant couldn't have pulled it off. *I'll show her,* Melanie vowed. Instead of climbing the fence at her usual spot and taking the path, she walked several yards along its perimeter, then climbed over and started off on a different route, cutting right through the thickest tangle of plants and trees.

To Melanie's untrained eye, the plants she trod on as she made her way along the new route looked like weeds. Any gardener could have told her, however, that they were all edible wild plants that sold for a fortune in health food stores.

"Look what you're doing, you horrible child!" Mrs. Crandall shrieked. The scraggly old woman appeared from nowhere and grabbed Melanie by the wrist. "You're trampling my plants!" Terrified, Melanie twisted and tugged, trying to wriggle out of Mrs. Crandall's grasp.

"Oh, no, you don't," Mrs. Crandall threatened and tightened her hold. "We're going to see what your parents have to say about this!"

At the mention of her parents, Melanie got really scared. Her mother and father had both warned her that if they received even one more complaint from Mrs. Crandall she'd be grounded for a month.

"No, please!" Melanie pleaded as Mrs. Crandall dragged her back toward her parents' house. "I'll never do it again. I promise."

"What good is a promise from a child like you?" Mrs. Crandall said. Melanie could feel that her silver-linked charm bracelet with her initial on it made it difficult for

Mrs. Crandall to keep a tight hold. Giving one mighty yank, she managed to pull free and back out of Mrs. Crandall's reach, leaving the old woman holding the bracelet, now broken.

"You'd better give my bracelet back," Melanie snarled. "I'll tell Mom and Dad you stole it if you don't."

Mrs. Crandall looked at the bracelet thoughtfully.

"It's worth a lot of money," Melanie continued. "I saved my allowance for a whole year to buy it."

"It took me a year to grow the plants you killed," Mrs. Crandall replied. "I think I ought to keep the bracelet in payment, don't you?"

Melanie couldn't believe her ears. How could any stupid plants be as valuable as her bracelet? "My mom and dad told me you're crazy!" she shouted. "They're right—you *are* crazy! You're crazy, crazy, crazy! I wish you and all your stupid old plants would die, you crazy old witch!"

"What did you call me?" Mrs. Crandall asked.

"A witch! That's what you are. I've seen you cooking your old weeds in that pot behind your house. I've seen the weird things you do." Melanie stood there glaring defiantly at Mrs. Crandall.

The old woman frowned and fixed the girl with an icy look. "You're a rude, undisciplined child. If I were you, I'd go home now before I . . ." She finished the sentence not with words but with a shake of her fist.

Suddenly, the last place on earth that Melanie wanted to be was on Mrs. Crandall's property. Whirling on her heels, she started running back toward home. Behind her, she could hear Mrs. Crandall shout, "Tell your parents I'll come by after dinner!"

All through dinner that night, Melanie listened for the sound of the doorbell. *Would Mrs. Crandall really come over?* she wondered. Just as she and her parents were finishing dessert, the doorbell rang.

"Who do you suppose that is?" Melanie's mother asked.

"I'll go see," her father offered.

Please don't let it be Mrs. Crandall, Please don't let it be Mrs. Crandall, Melanie chanted in her mind. She watched anxiously as her father left the room. The stern look he gave her when he returned, followed by Mrs. Crandall, told Melanie she was in big trouble. The old woman was carrying a box filled with the plants Melanie had trampled.

"Are you responsible for this?" Melanie's father asked as he lowered the box so that she could see inside.

Melanie pretended she'd never seen the destroyed plants. "What are they?" she asked.

"The plants you killed when you cut through Mrs. Crandall's yard today," her father replied, irritation dripping from his voice.

Melanie put on her most innocent expression. "I haven't been anywhere near Mrs. Crandall's yard," she lied. "It must have been somebody else."

"I saw you myself," Mrs. Crandall objected.

Melanie turned her most winning look on her father. "Really, Dad, it wasn't me."

Mrs. Crandall pulled Melanie's bracelet out of her pocket. "Are you saying this isn't your bracelet?"

"I've never seen it before," Melanie said quickly. "It looks something like mine, but that's not it."

84

Mrs. Crandall eyed Melanie coldly. "I wouldn't lie if I were you."

Melanie turned a pleading look on her father. "*She's* the one who's lying, Dad, not me."

Mrs. Crandall stiffened as if she'd just been hit in the stomach. Turning to Melanie's parents, she hissed, "No one has ever called me a liar. No one. From now on, keep your daughter off my property, or you'll all be sorry." Red with fury, the old woman stormed out.

Amazed by the extent of Mrs. Crandall's rage, Melanie's mother picked a withered-looking sprig out of the box of plants Melanie's father was holding and sighed, "Surely these plants aren't worth all of this fuss." Examining the sprig closer, she frowned. "This is bella donna, I'm sure of it. I think it might be poisonous."

Melanie saw her chance to get back at Mrs. Crandall. "She has all kinds of weird stuff growing in her yard. Probably lots of it is poison." Now that she was going, she couldn't stop. "I've even seen piles of dead rats all over her property."

"Dead rats?!" her parents blurted.

"Yeah," Melanie went on, really wound up. "And there's all kinds of junk piled up. Who knows what's living in there?"

"This sounds like something the health department should look into," Melanie's mother declared.

The next afternoon, a health department vehicle was parked in Mrs. Crandall's driveway. Melanie stood on the street and watched with delight as a man in an official-looking uniform systematically toured Mrs. Crandall's property writing citations for health violations. Mrs.

Crandall followed him, gesturing angrily with each scratch of his pen. Finally, when the man was finished, and she walked him to the gate, she noticed Melanie standing across the street watching them. The look of hatred the old woman gave Melanie chilled her to the bone.

———

THE NEXT THREE weeks were a nightmare for Melanie.

"But I didn't mean to do it," Melanie sobbed as her mother crouched on the floor picking up the pieces of her favorite ceramic figurine.

"Melanie, how can you say that?" her mother scolded. "I saw you deliberately throw it down the stairs! This is the third incident this week. I don't know what's come over you."

"I'm sorry. I'm really, really sorry," Melanie mumbled, as the tears kept rolling down her cheeks. "I can't seem to stop myself. Do you think I'm going crazy?"

Hearing the anguish in her daughter's voice, Mrs. Owens set aside the pieces of the figurine and pulled Melanie close to her. "No, you're not going crazy," she reassured her. "But maybe seeing a doctor wouldn't be a bad idea." Cupping Melanie's chin in her hand, she studied her daughter's tear-stained face. "How about it? Before things get worse?"

"Okay," Melanie agreed miserably, thinking secretly, *How could things get worse?*

That afternoon, she found out.

Melanie herself couldn't believe what she had done when her father grabbed the paintbrush out of her hand and shouted, "What do you think you're doing, young lady?!"

The Witch

Melanie stared at the garage wall in disbelief. The entire surface was covered with her signature scrawled in huge, paintbrushed letters. "Daddy, what's happening to me?" she cried, then burst into tears. "Make me stop!" she wailed. "Make me stop!"

Mr. Owens hugged his daughter close. "Maybe the doctor can help, sweetheart," he said reassuringly. "She'll probably know exactly what we need to do."

Melanie nodded, but deep down, she knew this wasn't something a doctor could cure.

THE DOCTOR RAN a series of tests on Melanie, then sent her back home with her parents to wait for the results. To cheer Melanie up, her parents invited her cousin, Kristin, to come for a visit.

It was Kristin who accidentally helped Melanie discover what was wrong. Melanie was pouring bubble bath crystals into her father's fish pond when Kristin ran out of the house and stopped her.

"Melanie, stop it!" she shouted. "You'll kill the fish!" She grabbed the bubble bath crystals out of Melanie's hands, and shook her cousin by the shoulders. "Snap out of it," she said.

"Snap out of it?" Melanie repeated as if in a daze.

"Yeah," Kristin replied. "It's like you're in a trance or something."

Suddenly, Melanie had her answer. "That's it, Kristin. That's why I've been doing these crazy things. Our neighbor's a witch. She got mad at me and probably put a spell on me."

"Don't be silly," her cousin scoffed. "There're no such things as witches."

Melanie shook her head. "You haven't met Mrs. Crandall."

MELANIE'S FRIEND, CELESTE, knew everything about witches. "It must be the bracelet," she said to Melanie, nodding, after Melanie had finished her story. "I don't know exactly what kind of spell she used or anything, but I know a witch has to have something that belongs to the person they want to control."

"What do I have to do to break the spell?" Melanie wanted to know.

"Can you get the bracelet back?" Celeste asked.

Melanie didn't see how she could.

"Then you'll have to kill the witch," Celeste stated with finality.

Melanie was shocked. "I can't kill Mrs. Crandall!"

"Yeah, guess you can't," Celeste agreed. "Then you'll just have to get your bracelet."

Melanie decided to steal her bracelet back that evening. She and her parents would hear the results of the doctor's tests in the morning, and after that, who knew what would happen. She knew Mrs. Crandall always did her marketing on Thursday night. It *had* to be tonight.

Melanie watched from her window until she saw Mrs. Crandall leave her house. Then, taking care so that her parents wouldn't hear her, she slipped out of her house into the shadows.

I should have made Celeste come with me, Melanie

thought as she crept through the snarl of vegetation on Mrs. Crandall's property. At night the shadows of the overgrown plants gave the whole place an alarmingly demonic look. Her heart pounding, Melanie almost turned back several times, but each time, she reminded herself she had to go on. She had to have that bracelet.

The only light Mrs. Crandall had left burning in her house was in the kitchen. Melanie circled the house twice looking for a way in before noticing that a heavy door at the bottom of an outside stairwell was slightly ajar. A faint light seeped out from inside. *This must be a basement,* Melanie thought. She stepped onto the first step. A twig snapped behind her. Frightened, Melanie gasped and shrank back. An instant later, a cat skittered past. Relieved, Melanie hurried down the steps to the door, pushed it open, and slipped inside.

The earthy smell inside the basement was almost over-whelming. The entire floor was covered with fungi—more different kinds of mushrooms than Melanie had known existed. Herbariums lined the walls and the special grow lights in them shed a ghoulish, yellow-green cast over every-thing. A board walkway leading through the mushrooms to a flight of wooden steps led into the crabby old woman's house. Melanie hurried across to the stairs and climbed up to the door leading into the main part of the house. She paused there for a moment, then held her breath and turned the knob. The door opened without a sound.

The first thing Melanie saw as she stepped into the kitchen was a roaring fire in an old wood stove. Something was boiling in a kettle on the front burner, filling the room with a foul odor. Melanie held her nose and tiptoed into the room. Strange dried plants and bits and pieces of who knows what hung on lines criss-crossed along the ceiling. Other weird-looking messes in bowls dotted the counters. There was no sign of her bracelet.

Melanie crept over to another door and pushed it open. The light from the kitchen spilled in, filling the dark adjoining room with spooky shadows. Melanie could just make out shelves filled with evil-looking masks and bunches of dried plants. Eyeing the collection with a mixture of awe and horror, she flicked on her pocket flashlight, and forced herself to go in.

Just being in that room gave Melanie goosebumps. Now that the kitchen door was closed, the only light in the room was her tiny flashlight beam. As she played it over the shelves, she could see skulls and bones lying among the masks and dried plants. *She really is a witch,* Melanie thought. A shiver went down her spine. Moving on, she shined her light into a corner.

"Agh," Melanie gasped. Hanging by their necks from wires in front of her were faceless wax dolls of all sizes and types. In the light from the flashlight, their pale bodies cast odd shadows on the wall behind them. They were frightening enough, but what chilled Melanie down to the bone was a special doll—a doll that *did* have a face—a face exactly like hers! Melanie froze when she saw it. The doll was hanging with the others, but slightly off by itself. The likeness was so exact it was scary…and around its neck was Melanie's bracelet.

"My bracelet!" Melanie exclaimed. Gingerly, she picked up the replica of herself and tried to unfasten the bracelet. The catch was locked. Melanie yanked, trying to

pull off the bracelet, but it held fast. She yanked again, harder. Suddenly, the door opened behind her. Light from the kitchen flooded the room.

"Melanie Owens!" a voice thundered.

Terrified, Melanie whirled around. Mrs. Crandall was hurrying toward her. She made a grab for Melanie, but Melanie dodged out of her reach. Holding the doll close, she ran for the kitchen.

"Stop! Stop!" Mrs. Crandall shouted, hurrying after her.

Running into the kitchen, Melanie raced for the basement door and tried to yank it open, but the latch was stuck. Mrs. Crandall grabbed the back of her jacket and held on tight. "Give me the doll!" she demanded. "Give it to me!"

Melanie squirmed and wriggled, trying to free herself. It was no use. "Here, take the stupid doll," she cried and threw it.

"No!" Mrs. Crandall gasped. Letting go of Melanie, she rushed to catch the doll. Melanie grabbed the basement doorknob and this time it turned. Behind her, Mrs. Crandall cried out as the doll fell feet first into the boiling pot and sizzled as it began to melt.

When Melanie tried to run down the stairs, somehow, she couldn't. Something funny was happening to her feet. Looking down, she saw little puddles forming at the end of her legs. Then her legs started to liquefy. *I'm melting just like that doll,* she thought wonderingly. Then the doll's body and head were melting, and Melanie discovered she couldn't think another thought.

HYDE AND SEEK

By Robert C. Welch

HEY, PETE! WHAT are you doing? Do you want to go down to the lot?"

Peter ignored his older brother, Mark, for a moment as he carefully glued the glowing skull to the skeleton's neck. It had to sit just right, or the movable jaw wouldn't be able to open.

"Pete!" his brother called again. Then he stomped into Peter's bedroom. "Geez. Are you still working on that thing?"

"Shh," Peter whispered as he settled the plastic skull on the tiny vertebrae. When he was convinced it would stick he looked up.

"Man, you spend way too much time on these stupid models," Mark pronounced. "Come on, it's the weekend! Brian, Al, and I are gonna go down to the lot and make a track for our bikes."

Peter glanced around his room. He could understand Mark's comment, even if he didn't agree with it. There was not one inch of level space that didn't have a plastic model on it. Vampires, werewolves, grotesque monsters, aliens— it was like some sort of museum of fright. Lately, he had even begun to hang models from the ceiling until he could get another bookshelf.

"Well?" Mark prompted. "Are you coming or not?"

"I was going to go down to the hobby shop," Peter answered. "Maybe I'll meet you guys afterwards."

"Oh, no," Mark groaned. "Tell me you're not going to buy *another* model."

"I'm just going to take a look," Peter protested. "I'll meet you guys at the lot."

"All right. Catch you later."

Peter checked the skeleton one last time before riding to his second home, The Toy Box Game and Hobby Shop. The grinning skull sat solidly on the neck.

"Perfect," Peter said. He moved the model to a spot he had cleared on a shelf, and took off.

MR. PISLING, THE owner of The Toy Box, was Peter's hero. He was as old as Peter's grandfather, but he knew more about toys and models than any other kid Peter knew.

"Hi, Mister Pisling," Peter greeted as he pushed open the door of the shop. "Just taking a quick look to see if anything new came in."

"As a matter of fact, I'm unloading a box of stuff I got this morning," Mr. Pisling said, motioning Peter to follow him as he ducked behind the curtain that separated the stockroom from the rest of the shop.

"Where's it from?" Peter asked, following the old man into the back.

Mr. Pisling grinned. "Good question. Actually, I'm not sure. My cousin wrote me saying that she knew of an old magic and novelty store that was closing down, so I told her to send me anything that looked interesting."

He knelt down over a huge box that was sitting on the floor. It had already been opened, and Styrofoam bubbles covered the floor. Peter examined the items that had already been unpacked. It looked like a lot of junk to him. Mostly old magic props, some stupid board games, and rubber body parts.

"Ah ha!" Mr. Pisling exclaimed, his voice muffled by the box as he reached in to grab something from the bottom. He pulled out a dusty carton. "What have we here?" He handed it to Peter. "Looks like it might be right up your alley, boyo."

Peter took the carton and blew off the dust. "Cool!" he cried. The cover of the box showed a pretty girl screaming in terror as she backed away from a scary figure. The artwork looked like some old magazines his dad had from the fifties, but the bright colors were faded and the bold writing was barely legible.

"The unfortunate Dr. Jekyll and the monstrous Mr. Hyde," Peter read out loud, "captured in this incredibly detailed model of the infamous duo." He gently pulled off the box top, peered inside, and frowned.

"What's wrong?" Mr. Pisling asked.

"Look. Someone busted it up." Peter poked his finger at the bits of plastic in the box. It was clear to his experienced eye that the model had actually been assembled at one point, and then been broken to pieces. "Looks like it was a pretty neat model, too," he concluded dejectedly.

"Tell you what," the old man said briskly. "I'm never going to be able to sell it like this. Why don't you take it home and see if you can do something with it."

"Really?" Peter asked.

"Sure. If *you* can't repair it then it can't be done."

"Thanks, Mister Pisling!" Peter said, pumping the store owner's outstretched hand. He shoved the box top back on, ran out the door, and jumped on his bike. All thoughts of the vacant lot vanished from his mind.

When he got home, he ran up to his room and carefully spread out the pieces of his new project. He could see it was going to be a challenge. Some of the parts had broken at the glue joint—those would be easy. But others were broken in the middle of the piece, and the plastic looked as if it had been twisted. To top it off, there were no longer any instructions for assembly. Gathering his brushes, glues, and solvents, Peter set to work.

"What happened to you?" Mark's voice came so suddenly from behind him that Peter jumped. As he did he sliced his thumb on the sharp edge of one of the pieces.

"Ouch!" he yelled as a bright red line of blood appeared and smeared Mr. Hyde's head. Setting down the bloody head, Peter whirled on his brother. "Don't ever sneak up on me like that!"

Mark rolled his eyes. "You were so busy you just didn't hear me. What are you working on? Mom says you've been up here all day."

Peter looked at his watch. Mark was right. He'd spent the whole day working on Dr. Jekyll and Mr. Hyde.

"Mister Pisling gave me a really neat model to work on," he answered, waving at the tiny body parts that cluttered his desktop. "It's a really old one that was all busted up. Mister Pisling wants to see if I can fix it."

A drop of vivid red blood splashed onto the piece of plastic Peter had identified as the model's torso. He yanked back his thumb and got up angrily. "And look what you made me do!"

Mark pushed himself away from the door, shaking his head. "Don't blame me. Maybe it was the monster that did it." Laughing, he walked down the hall.

Still upset with his brother, Peter went to the bathroom and wrapped a bandage around his cut thumb. Then he grabbed a tissue and returned to clean off the pieces. Oddly, though, he could not find any trace of his blood on the plastic.

By the time his mother called him for dinner, Peter had nearly finished reassembling the broken model. The finished product did not quite live up to the box-top picture, but it wasn't too bad. The "incredibly detailed model" was a man with interchangeable heads. The slightly nerdy Dr. Jekyll and the snarling, animal face of Mr. Hyde. Peter automatically set Dr. Jekyll's head to one side.

"Peter!" his mother called a second time. "We're going to start without you."

"Coming!" Peter yelled back. He quickly glued the last piece—an upraised arm with a bloody knife gripped in its hand—and stuck it to the creature's body. He held it for a moment to let the glue fix.

"Peter!" his father called. "Last time!"

Peter held the model together a moment longer, then raced downstairs.

He gulped down his dinner like a starving man, anxious to get back to his room to study his finished project. But his excitement quickly turned to despair when he saw the figure. The glue holding the monster's arm hadn't held properly, and the upraised knife was now resting at Mr. Hyde's side. Peter tugged glumly at the arm.

"Oh, great," he muttered. The glue had, of course, set perfectly by this time and the arm remained immobile in its new position. Peter briefly considered snapping it off, but figured the model had received enough abuse.

Still, he felt very pleased with his results. The model looked as good as new, and even he had trouble seeing some of the lines where he'd joined parts together. He took the model downstairs to occupy a place of honor on top of the television set. That lasted most of the evening, but when he went to bed his mother made him take "that gruesome thing" with him. He set it carefully on his desk and climbed into bed.

———————

PETER DIDN'T KNOW what woke him up, but he could see by his clock it was almost three in the morning. Ghastly glowing skulls and terrifying monsters stared down at him from around the room as he tried to place the sound he had heard. When it didn't repeat, he fell back asleep.

He woke up later, with the morning sun shining brightly into his room. He stretched and stood lazily, glancing over at his desk.

"That's odd," he murmured. His eyebrows drew together in a puzzled frown as he took a step closer. The model of Mr. Hyde was resting crookedly on top of something. He picked it up and saw the broken head of Dr. Jekyll.

"I can't believe you did that," he said to the model. "I could've sworn there was nothing there when I put you down." He picked up the pieces of Dr. Jekyll's head. That explained the noise he had heard last night—it must have been the crack of the new glue giving way.

"Oh, well," he said, tossing the ruined pieces in the wastebasket.

That morning Peter's parents decided to take the family out for breakfast. While they were driving, Mark turned to Peter. "Oh, by the way, that was a good one last night."

"What?"

"You know, I wasn't going to say anything, but I decided to let you know I saw it so you won't be surprised when your turn comes."

"What are you talking about?" Peter asked.

Mark just looked at him as if to say he wasn't being fooled by Peter's act. "You know, the model? Propped on my nightstand? Very funny."

"Mark, I have no clue what you're talking about."

"Right? I suppose Doctor Jekyll—"

"Mr. Hyde," Peter corrected.

"Whatever. I suppose he got tired of standing on your desk so he decided to come see what my room was like?"

"I don't know what you mean," Peter protested.

Mark held up a hand. "All right. Okay. So you don't know anything about it. Fine."

Peter sat in the back seat and stared out the window. He was still trying to figure out what Mark had been talking about when they got back home.

Storm, the family dog, almost knocked down Peter's father when he opened the door. The poor dog's nose was all bloody, and he was very excited about something.

"Wow!" Mark said when he saw the deep gashes in

the dog's nose. "That must have been some cat."

"I'll check outside to see if the poor thing is still out there," Peter's mother said. "Mark and Peter, I want you two to scout out any bloodstains on the walls or floor and clean them up."

Peter found some drops on the stairs, and a smear on the wall of the hallway. *What was that stupid dog doing?* he wondered. *I thought dogs slept all day.*

He scrubbed the bloodstains and checked his parent's bedroom. It was clean, as was Mark's room. Then he checked in his room.

The new model was standing on his nightstand streaked with blood. Ignoring the shivery little tingles along his spine, Peter bent over to pick up the model. The tingling spread to his arms and neck as he saw the fresh blood smeared on the knife in Mr. Hyde's hand.

"That's crazy," he whispered, dismissing the ridiculous thoughts forming in his head. Still, how did the model get on the nightstand? He clearly remembered leaving it on his desk when he had left that morning.

Peter dropped the model on his bed and quickly wiped up the dog's blood. Then he went to find Mark.

His brother was trying to get a bloody noseprint out of the carpet. Peter knelt down and said in a low voice, "Mark. I need you to do me a favor."

Something in his voice made his brother look at him strangely. "What is it?"

"Tell me exactly what happened last night when you saw the model in your room." Peter could see his brother beginning to make some joke and he quickly put up his hand. "Please, Mark. Just tell me."

"Okay," Mark said slowly. "I admit you got a good jump out of me. I heard some noise and when I turned over there was that stupid model practically staring me in the face. It didn't help that my clock lit it up and made it look all red and gruesome. Anyway, after catching my breath I said, 'Peter, if that thing isn't gone by the time I look again I'm going to break every single one of your models.'"

"And?" Peter whispered.

"And you know as well as I do!" Mark snapped.

"No, I don't," Peter insisted.

Mark sighed. "Okay," he said, obviously still not believing Peter. "Then I heard you chuckle."

Peter rocked back on his heels and sat down hard. "Mark, I don't know what I can say to make you believe me, but I swear I was nowhere near your room last night."

His brother was looking at him very strangely. "Look, if you're sorry just say so."

"Fine, don't believe me." Peter scrambled to his feet. "I gotta go to the hobby store."

He ran upstairs and grabbed the model of Mr. Hyde. Stuffing it into his book bag, he raced back downstairs and out to the garage. He hopped on his bike and took off down the street.

"HI-YO, PETEY!" Mr. Pisling said enthusiastically. "How's the restoration project?"

"It's done," Peter said, pulling the model out of his bag.

"So fast? Let me take a look at that." Mr. Pisling brought the model closer for examination. "That's incredible. I can't

even see where you fastened the pieces together."

"Actually," Peter said, "I want to give it back to you."

"But why? I gave it to you."

"Well, seeing as it's so old and all," he searched for more explanations, "and I already have a model of Mr. Hyde from a newer kit."

Mr. Pisling shrugged. "Tell you what. I'll keep it here on display, so everyone can see it." He placed the model prominently in the front window. "How's that?"

"Great idea, Mister Pisling," Peter said, slightly relieved. He waved to the kind old man and left, feeling much better than he had on the way over.

The next day at school Peter didn't tell anyone about his weird experience, and by the time he got home, he had almost forgotten it.

"Oh, Pete," his mother said when he opened the front door. "I'm so sorry."

"About what?" he asked, confused.

"It was just on the radio," his father said. "Mister Pisling was found dead in his store."

Peter's stomach seemed to roll over slowly and sink to his knees. He paused, shrugging off his book pack. "What? I mean, how?"

His father glanced quickly at Peter's mom. "They think it was robbery," he said quietly. "Mister Pisling was stabbed, son. I'm sorry."

The room seemed to tilt on its side, and Peter felt his lunch making its way back up his throat. He turned suddenly and ran back outside. He heard his mother call after him, but he ignored her as he leapt on his bike and sped away.

Peter knew where he was going, even if he didn't

want to admit it to himself. But as he approached the darkened windows of Mr. Pisling's shop, padlocked and roped off with yellow police tape, Peter didn't quite know what he was expecting. He looked around, then carefully slipped under the tape and walked slowly to the display window. The afternoon sun illuminated only motes of dust where the model of Mr. Hyde had stood. Peter knew then that he had let something loose, and he had no idea where it was or how to stop it.

Peter slowly climbed on his bike and headed home. Thinking of poor Mr. Pisling, he didn't feel the model ease its way out of his book bag, raising its knife for its next victim.

DREAM CATCHER

By Anne Bancroft Fowler

RAVEN SCOLLCROFT OPENED his backpack and dumped the contents onto his sleeping bag. The dream catcher took a bounce and floated away, like a Frisbee borne on a breath of summer air.

Raven grabbed for it, hoping no one else had seen, but he was too late. Twelve pairs of curious eyes watched it go up, then start to drift lazily down.

"What is that thing?" Raven's new friend, Marc, asked in a puzzled voice.

The Scout troop was out for the weekend, camping overnight on the shores of Lake Superior. When Raven's grandmother had heard about the trip, she'd insisted on giving him her own personal dream catcher to take along. "You must use it there," she warned. "Powerful spirits walk those woods."

"Hey, Raven!" Kurt snatched the dream catcher out of the air and held it out of reach. Its feathers ruffled in the morning breeze. "What'cha got there?"

"Just give it back, Kurt." Raven clutched at it in vain.

"In a minute! Let me take a look!" Kurt held the webbed circle to his eye and peered through an inch-wide hole in the middle. "What is this, some kind of Indian charm?" Kurt shifted the feathered treasure to a position above his head and he hopped from one foot to the other, in an imitation of Indians he had seen in the movies. Some of the Scouts laughed.

It made Raven want to deck them all, but it was too late. His secret was out. He could look forward to another summer of kids like Kurt putting him down with their ignorant stereotypes.

Raven had been teased about his name as long as he could remember. And when people learned of his Native American ancestry, it always got worse. He was only part Indian, and during the winter he lived in the city with his white father, where he conveniently ignored his heritage. But summers he spent with his Grandmother Noko, one of the few remaining full-blooded Ojibwa Indians. She lived on the reservation and followed the old ways, as did most of her friends.

"Back off, Kurt," Marc said, coming to Raven's support.

Raven grabbed Kurt's arm and tore the dream catcher from his hand. They stood glaring at each other.

"Break it up, boys. We're here to learn about the outdoors." Mr. Johnson, the Scout leader, came out of the woods and dumped an armload of firewood on the ground. "Kurt, see if you can get this fire going, and Raven, I need you and Marc to help me set up the archery target."

"Okay," Raven mumbled. A smirking Kurt moved away from him. Raven examined the dream catcher carefully. No feathers were missing, as far as he could tell. Grandmother Noko would never forgive him if he brought it back damaged. It had been careless of him to dump his pack out with a bully like Kurt standing by.

He smoothed the catcher and put it back in his pack before he ran to where Marc and Mr. Johnson stood waiting in the clearing. Together they set up the archery target, then Mr. Johnson sent Raven and Marc back to the campsite for bows and arrows.

"Well?" Marc asked as soon as they were out of earshot.

"Well, what?" Raven said defiantly.

"How come you didn't tell me about that thing? I thought we were friends." He paused and pointed to Raven's backpack. "What is that thing you have in there, anyway?"

Raven sighed. "That *thing* belongs to my Grandmother Noko. She's very superstitious."

Marc looked puzzled. "What's it supposed to do?"

"Noko thinks the night is filled with dreams, so she keeps her dream catcher hanging by the bed to catch them as they float by. The good dreams get through the hole in the center, and the bad dreams get tangled up in the feathers and disappear the next morning."

"She really believes that?"

Raven shrugged. "She believes a lot of strange things. It's hard to explain."

"What about you?" Marc asked, with a slight smile on his face.

Raven shook his head. "Are you kidding? Of course not!"

Some of Noko's ideas did make sense to Raven. At least, he could understand why she believed in them . . . but a dream catcher? He didn't think so.

The rest of the morning went by peacefully, filled with woodcrafts and nature study. The troop hiked to the top of a waterfall in the afternoon, and that night they roasted hot dogs and marshmallows over the open campfire.

After clean-up, Mr. Johnson took Raven aside. "I heard Kurt teasing you earlier," he said, eyeing him thoughtfully. "Don't ever be ashamed of who you are, Raven." Then he returned to his seat by the fire and gathered the troop around him.

"Lake Superior plays a big part in the history of this area," Mr. Johnson told the other boys. "Did you know that the shores of Gitche Gumee in the first line of Longfellow's poem *The Song of Hiawatha*, refers to Lake Superior?"

Mr. Johnson droned on, but Raven didn't hear a word he said. He knew Indian lore inside out and backwards from listening to his grandmother. His head spun with stories of Gitche Manitou, the Great Spirit, and Manabozho, the son of the West Wind. That was all Grandmother Noko ever talked about, and he pretended to be interested. But the truth was, they were nonsense to him, no better than fairy tales.

Finally Mr. Johnson finished his tale on Native American history and announced it was time for lights out. Raven was glad. He zipped into his sleeping bag next to Marc and immediately started to drift off to sleep.

"You awake?" Marc asked.

Raven yawned. "Barely."

"Well, I was wondering what you did with your grandmother's dream catcher."

Raven opened one eye. "I put it away. Why? You want

to use it?" The boys laughed together. "I don't like being made fun of," Raven said, by way of explanation. "So nobody's going to see that thing again...at least not on this trip." he added, unaware of how he would soon come to regret his decision.

NO SOONER HAD Raven fallen asleep than he began to dream. It was night, but the moon lit his path as he ran through the forest where the Scout troop had hiked earlier that day. He was alone, his feet skimming silently over the ground without disturbing a leaf. Coming to the edge of a clearing, he paused to stare at a small herd of grazing deer.

Automatically, he dropped his bow from his shoulder and reached behind his head to draw an arrow from his quiver. Then he stopped and looked down at himself in surprise, suddenly aware that he was dressed in traditional Indian garb, with a bow and arrow in his hand.

I'm dreaming, he told himself within the dream. *And it's a happy dream, the kind of good dream Grandmother Noko caught in her dream catcher.* With a little laugh, he quickly placed the arrow in the bow and took careful aim. Then it happened.

A shadow fell across the grass, like a dark cloud passing before the moon. Startled, the herd of deer looked up, pranced a few steps in alarm, then darted off in every direction.

Raven lowered his bow in disappointment. He gazed up at the heavens, trying to determine the size of the cloud. *Would the deer return when it had passed?* he wondered.

The dream continued, but the content was clearly beginning to change.

Suddenly, an enormous figure lumbered onto the scene. It towered over the clearing and completely blocked out the sky. Raven recoiled in his sleep and tried to wake himself up. Standing erect on two legs like a man, the beast had the head of a wild boar, with sharp, tusklike fangs jutting from its lower jaw. Its immense, bear-shaped body was covered with fur. From its clawed hands, jagged sparks of electricity shot forth like lightning bolts.

"Raven!" the beast called to him. "I have come to teach you your fate. It does you no honor to lie hidden in the trees," it growled. "Come into the clearing where I can talk to you!"

Frightened, Raven dropped his bow and arrow and turned to run.

"Stop!" the beast commanded.

Raven ran all the faster, but not fast enough to escape the bolt of blue ice that sizzled from the monster's claw. It was a huge jolt of power that penetrated Raven's heart, knocking him to his knees. He gasped for breath and collapsed, feeling himself slipping into unconsciousness.

When Raven awoke, he was confused and painfully aware of the cold that enveloped him like a shroud. He turned his head from side to side, slowly realizing that he was at the campsite. The fire was almost out, but in the dying embers Raven could see the sleeping figures of the Scouts around him.

"Wow, what a dream," he murmured as he rooted deeper into his sleeping bag, shivering. His teeth began to chatter. *It's summer!* he thought. *Why am I so cold?*

Then he remembered the dream. Sitting up with a start, he felt strange and lightheaded. He tried to wiggle his feet and discovered that he couldn't feel his toes...or his fingers. *What's wrong with me?* he wondered, beginning to feel frightened.

He looked at his hands, turning them over, examining them...seeing right through them!

Terrified, Raven cried out in alarm, but only a rush of wind came from his mouth. *What's happening?* his mind shouted as he felt his spirit begin to drift upward toward the treetops. His spirit body, now transparent, was actually floating several feet above his solid body, which was still lying on the ground. Panicked, he called upon the one person who might know what to do. *Grandmother Noko!* he shouted in the silence of his spirit. *Help me!*

Immediately his grandmother's image appeared to him in a shower of light. "Raven!" she cried, dropping to one knee beside his solid body on the ground. "What have you done?"

Raven watched his grandmother pull back the flap of his sleeping bag to reveal his chest. Silently she pointed to the area around his heart. His chest had become as transparent as clear ice, and Raven could see that his heart was blue and covered with frost, not beating.

"Tell me what happened," his grandmother commanded.

Raven told her of his dream. She nodded wisely. "An evil spirit, a Windigo, has turned your heart to ice," she said. "I warned you to use the dream catcher. Why did you not listen?"

Raven's voice trembled with fear. "I'm sorry,

Grandmother. Tell me what to do."

"There is only the old way. You must journey to the cave of the Windigo and steal some hot tallow from its candle. It will melt the ice in your heart and restore you to life. Hurry! To succeed, the act must be completed before the light of day touches your body." As she spoke, his grandmother quickly untied a length of slender rope from around her waist and thrust it toward Raven.

"Take this," she said. "It will aid you in your quest."

"Wait!" Raven cried. "Where are you going? I need your help."

"I have done all I can. I am old and must return to my body before the life force is spent," she said. "Remember, concentrate on securing the tallow to rub on your heart. Allow nothing to distract you from your task, else all will be lost."

Raven was frightened. "But what should I do? How will I find the Windigo?"

"Call on your namesake, the Raven," his grandmother said, as she began to fade. "His instinct can guide you, if you will but heed it."

As Raven watched, Grandmother Noko dissolved before his eyes, leaving only the smallest residue of light where she had appeared.

Raven didn't understand the strange command, but he was determined to obey the wise old woman. He tried to concentrate on the bird for whom he was named. *Raven*, he said in his mind. *Raven, Raven, Raven.*

Suddenly he heard a great flapping of wings. An enormous black bird, larger than a man, swooped down from the sky. It landed on the ground a few feet away. *Why have you called me?* The bird's voice rang in Raven's thoughts. Frightened, Raven didn't answer at once, and the great bird began to gather its wings beneath it for flight.

Wait! Raven shouted in his mind. *I need your help!* He quickly told the giant bird all that his grandmother had told him, and at the bird's command, he climbed upon the raven's broad wings.

Looking down on the forest below as they rose into the sky, Raven realized that his spirit body had become one with that of the great bird. And, now, in the form of the bird itself, Raven circled once to get his bearings. Then, following his instincts as Grandmother Noko had advised, he flew directly north, toward the land of perpetual ice and snow.

Vast stands of timber and great waterfalls dotted the landscape below, as Raven soared through the sky. Then the vegetation began to change as he came upon snow-covered mountains. The trees were short and stubby, with scrubby clumps of needles growing from their stunted limbs.

Raven flew on. The air grew colder as he reached the edges of the glaciers, where huge sheets of ice covered the ground and had done so since before man walked the earth. Here Raven turned east, for he suddenly remembered from the many legends his grandmother had told him that the Windigo lived on a glacial island all his own.

THE MOON HAD begun to sink in the sky before Raven saw the entrance to the cave. Carved in a wall of ice, the hole was almost hidden beneath an overhanging cliff. *This is the home of the Windigo you seek.* Raven could hear his grand-mother's voice whisper in his mind, as clearly as if she were there. *Go there now. Save yourself.*

Separating his spirit from his carrier, Raven signaled the great bird to land on a narrow ledge directly above the hole. Once there, he lowered himself carefully down the face of the ice cliff by means of Grandmother Noko's rope and swung his legs into the hole.

As soon as he let go of the rope, he realized that there was no floor beneath his feet. He plunged through the darkness for several minutes before he hit bottom with a thud.

Immediately he sprang to his feet, then crouched, fearful of being discovered. Nothing happened. Not a breath of frigid air stirred to signal a waiting presence. The only sound he heard was a distant trickle of water, like the runoff of slowly melting ice. After a few moments, his eyes adjusted to the darkness, and Raven straightened up to look around.

He was standing in the center of a great ice chamber, a huge cavern that appeared to be several miles high and just as wide. Along the sides, he could see hundreds of crystalline blocks of ice, each square frozen around a dark-er core. Raven realized there was something oddly familiar to him about the shapes at the center of the blocks, but he had no time to examine them now. *Allow nothing to dis-tract you from your task,* he heard Grandmother Noko's warning echoing in his brain. *Else all will be lost.*

At the end of the great cavern, a tiny light flickered in the darkness. It looked like the flame of a candle, and Raven moved cautiously toward it.

Suddenly, he heard a thundering crash and felt the ice tremble beneath his feet. Terrified, Raven ran quickly to hide behind one of the ice statues. After a few seconds, a giant figure lumbered into sight, holding before it an enormous candelabra with twelve burning candles. It was the Windigo!

Crouching behind the block of ice, Raven watched, trembling, as the beast approached. It stopped a few short yards from where he hid. Holding the candelabra at an angle, the Windigo allowed a few drops of hot wax to fall from a candle onto one of the statues. Immediately, the icy outer shell melted away, and the body of a young Native American girl fell to the floor. Raven could see that her heart was encased in blue ice, just like his own in the body he had left by the campfire. But as the tallow hit the girl, her eyelids fluttered, and she began to regain consciousness.

In a flash, the Windigo tore a piece of flesh from her arm. The maiden screamed in horror and tried to pull away, but the Windigo ignored her. Holding the candelabra with one hand and dragging the terrified maiden behind it with the other, the Windingo began to tear her body apart, limb by limb, devouring the pieces as it walked back to the farthest reaches of the ice palace.

Raven remained concealed among the ice statues, shuddering. He now understood what fate awaited him if he could not get the hot tallow and make his way back to the camp before dawn.

He had lost all track of time, but he knew he must act quickly—his life depended on it. As soon as the Windigo disappeared in the distance, Raven ventured out from his hiding place and ran after the beast, who had vanished through a huge arched doorway of ice.

Reaching the archway, Raven stopped long enough to calm his racing mind, then cautiously stepped into the icy cave beyond. In the flickering candlelight, he could make out the figure of the giant resting its head on a table at the far end of the huge cavern. He started in that direction, then nearly collapsed with fright as he heard a deep rumbling.

Frozen in his tracks, Raven stared at the monster until it dawned on him that the beast had fallen asleep and was snoring! Creeping along the wall, shaking at each of the beast's thunderous snores, Raven finally approached the table. Standing on tiptoe, he reached for the heavy candelabra. It tipped in his grasp, causing a drop of hot tallow from the candle to spill onto the Windigo's furry skin.

"Aaargh!" the giant yelled in pain as it awoke. Looking around, the monster spotted Raven. It leaped up from the table with a roar, sending a bolt of blue lightning sizzling toward Raven's head.

Clutching the candelabra to his chest, Raven ran for his life. As he dodged between the ice blocks in the great cavern, bits of tallow from the candles splashed on the frozen forms. Instantly, their outer shells fell away, and figures emerged, moaning and crying for help. Roaring angrily, the giant paused in its pursuit of Raven long enough to blow its freezing breath on every stirring figure, turning each back into a frozen statue.

Panting with fear, Raven made it to the far end of the cavern—only to discover that there was no door, no exit from the cave. The hole through which he had fallen into the cavern was high above his head, too high for him to reach, and the wall was too steep and icy for him to climb.

He felt a tremor like an earthquake shake the ice beneath his feet and heard the heavy footsteps of the approaching beast. *Concentrate on a way to get out of here!* Raven told himself. He focused his whole mind on seeing himself astride the raven once more.

Suddenly, Grandmother Noko's rope miraculously slid down the ice wall beside him. Raven looked up. His namesake had received his silent message, for there, holding the rope firmly its beak, was the giant black bird. Quickly, Raven looped the rope around his waist and began to pull himself up the slippery ice, the candelabra still firmly in his grasp.

The Windigo was close behind. Raven felt its frigid breath on his neck as the beast's claws clutched at him. Turning to face his foe, Raven held the candelabra before him, thrusting it into the monster's face. The beast fell back with a horrified roar, as hot wax splattered on his skin, giving Raven just enough time to scramble up the ice wall to the waiting bird.

Outside the entrance, Raven rolled all the remaining tallow into a ball and stored it in his mouth before he once again climbed aboard to blend his spirit form with that of the great bird. Then he took flight, the tallow protected in his beak.

IT WAS ALMOST dawn as Raven looked down from the sky above the campfire. He saw that the Scouts were awake, gathered around Mr. Johnson, who administered CPR to Raven's still form. A stricken Marc knelt by his side.

A short distance away, the contents of Raven's back-pack lay scattered on the ground, and Kurt leaned over to pick up Grandmother Noko's dream catcher.

"No!" Raven screamed, seeing the dream catcher in Kurt's hand. His cry came out as the screech of a raucous bird. Kurt looked up in surprise.

"Don't touch that!" Raven shrieked again, diving on Kurt and flapping his great wings in an effort to drive him away from his grandmother's prize.

Kurt dropped the feathered object and backed away in alarm, but as Raven opened his beak to screech again, he could no longer hold the precious tallow in his beak, and it fell directly onto the dream catcher. It burst into a great ball of flame just as the sun broke over the horizon, its early rays touching the cold body of Raven Scollcroft.

And in that moment, the mortal Raven Scollcroft died. For without his grandmother's sacred dream catcher, there would be no return from the other world of his consciousness. He was trapped forever in the world of his dreams…and nightmares.

For more scary thrills,
read...

More Bone-Chilling
Tales of Fright